RUN TO THE ARK

D1422130

Run to the Ark is the fourth book in Tom McCaughren's award-winning series about that eternal fugitive of the countryside, the fox. A journalist and former broadcaster with RTÉ, Tom is a native of Ballymena, Co. Antrim. The other books in his fox series are *Run with the Wind*, *Run to Earth*, *Run Swift Run Free*, *Run to the Wild Wood* and *Run for Cover,* all published by Wolfhound Press, an imprint of Merlin Publishing. He has also written a number of adventure stories for young people and three novels for teenagers, including *Rainbows of the Moon*. His books have been translated into German, Swedish, Japanese, Korean, French, Dutch, Danish and Latvian.

Also published by TOM McCAUGHREN
From Wolfhound Press

The Fox Series
Book 1   Run with the Wind
Book 2   Run to Earth
Book 3   Run Swift Run Free
Book 4   Run to the Ark
Book 5   Run to the Wild Wood
Book 6   Run for Cover

Tom McCaughren's fox books have won many awards for literature, including: the Reading Association of Ireland Book Award 1985; the Irish Book Awards Medal 1987; the White Ravens selection 1988 (International Youth Library Munich); The Young Persons' Book of the Decade Award 1980–1990 (Irish Children's Book Trust); and the Oscar Wilde Society's Literary Recognition Award 1992. Contact www.tommccaughren.net for more information or www.merlinwolfhound.com

RUN TO
THE ARK

Tom McCaughren

WOLFHOUND PRESS

This edition published in 2007 by
WOLFHOUND PRESS
An Imprint of Merlin Publishing
Newmarket Hall, Cork Street
Dublin 8, Ireland
Tel: +353 1 4535 866
Fax: +353 1 4535 930
publishing@merlin.ie
www.merlinwolfhound.com

Text © 1991, 2007 Tom McCaughren
Editing, Design and Layout © 2007 Merlin Publishing
All rights reserved

ISBN 086327 3424 First paperback edition 1991
13-Digit ISBN 978-0-86327-941-6 Second paperback edition 2007
10-Digit ISBN 086327 9414

*This book is fiction. All characters, incidents and names have no connection with any
person living or dead. Any apparent resemblance is purely coincidental.*

A CIP catalogue record for this book is available from the British Library.

10 9 8 7 6 5 4 3 2 1

Typeset by Carrigboy Typesetting Services
Cover Design by Graham Thew Design
Cover Illustration by William Helps
Printed in Great Britain by Creative Print and Design.

To my father,
Jack McCaughren, for the things he taught
me about the ways of the wild.

'I set my bow in the cloud, and it shall be a token …
I will look upon it that I may remember the everlasting
covenant between God and every living creature …'

From the story of Noah and the Ark
(Genesis 9:13–16)

Contents

Foreword

The Bow in the Cloud appears above the Land of Sinna and the hard-pressed creatures of the valley see it as a sign. The fur-trapping crisis has now passed, but EC lamb production is at its height and the fox can only hunt in the sheep fields on pain of death. The badger is blamed for spreading tuberculosis in cattle and whole families are being destroyed in their setts. The otter finds his rivers are becoming more and more polluted, and decides it is time to go.

Somewhere beyond the bow, the otter tells his friends, lies a safe haven. But does it really exist or is it just a figment of his imagination? Thus starts a journey that is full of excitement and surprise, a journey that brings joy and sadness, fear and hope to a whole range of characters, some old, some new – characters like Whiskers, Old Sage Brush, Vickey, Hop-along, She-la, Stumpy, Snout, Sniff and many others . . .

ONE

Skeletons of Winter

The birch trees were bare and white like the bleached bones of winter. Crinkled strips of bark fluttered lifeless in the wind, while the topmost branches clawed the darkening sky like a creature drawing its last breath. Here and there black knots of twigs stood out like last season's nests, but no birds lived in this small grove of birches. This was the home of a fox. Or so it used to be . . .

The young vixen who nosed her way through the tufts of long withered grass around the base of the trees was puzzled. There was no scent of fox, at least none that she could detect. She lifted her fine muzzle into the wind and looked out across the vast expanse of bog. It was brown, barren and lifeless. No scent of animal or bird assailed her sensitive nose, no trace of her own kind that might have frightened them away.

Turning her back to the wind so that it burrowed down to the roots of her long red fur and flicked it towards her head, she set off towards the nearest fields. Carefully she picked her way around deep turf banks and brown peaty pools, looking up now and then to make sure she was still going in the right direction. It was an old fox who had shown her how to make this treacherous crossing with safety and, if need be, in the shortest possible time. The bog was his home, and he knew it like the back of his paw.

The vixen stopped and looked around once more. Where had he gone? she wondered. Because of his advanced years he rarely strayed far from the birches, for the bog provided him with all the food and safety he needed. Why then had she found no trace of him? Not even a sent that would suggest he had been there within the past day or two?

Strange, she thought, and stopped again. The brown peaty water began to ooze up around her paws. She raised her nose to read the wind. It was still blowing from behind her, eddying around the birches and the sloping fields and occasionally coming back towards her. She cocked her ears and twitched them around to catch any sound that might tell her if the old fox was near. There was none, only a deathly silence on the bog that instinctively made her wait and sift the signs in the wind.

Suddenly she stiffened, and she felt the hairs standing on her neck, not from the wind, but from a fear that came with a whiff of something she had caught in the wind. She sniffed once more. Whatever it was, it evaded her this time and she held her nose in the air waiting to pick it up again.

The wind plucked at her fur and swirled across her nostrils. There it was again. No mistake. A smell of death. She dropped to the ground, oblivious to the brown, peaty water that soaked her white underfur. Her heart was pounding and her mind was racing. She lowered her head and looked at the brown water that now covered her fore-paws, not seeing it and not wanting to accept the truth of what she knew. But there it was, stronger now, the smell of death. The smell of fox!

She felt a great urge to rise and run, but restrained herself. In one way she wanted to know if it was the old fox; in another way she didn't, for as long as she didn't know for certain, there was always the possibility that it wasn't him. Yet if it was, she just couldn't turn around and leave him.

The dirty water dripped from the soaked fur of her underbelly as she forced herself up and crept forward. The smell of death became a stench, choking her sensitive nostrils and confusing her mind. It was all she could do not to turn tail and leave the area with all possible speed.

The brittle heather still hid the corpse from view, and so strong was the smell now that she felt the old fox, if indeed that's who it was, must have been lying there for days. She dropped to the ground again, weighed down by an overwhelming sense of guilt, and reproached herself for not having called to see him more often. Had he suffered a painful death, a long lingering death? She wondered. Could she have helped him, perhaps have brought him food? Oh no, she thought, he didn't starve to death. He didn't, did he?

The thought compelled her to move, and she ran forward quickly, weaving in and around the humps of heather until at last she came to the source of the smell. She stopped, fully expecting now to see the decomposing body of the old fox. Instead, to her horror, she saw the bodies of many foxes. They were lying at the edge of the bog, some heaped one upon the other, the white of their upturned bellies testifying to the fact that they were dead.

The vixen looked around. There was no sign of man, although this, she thought bitterly, was clearly his work. She edged closer to the mound of death. Two or three of the foxes lay on their sides in the peaty water, submerged except for one black ear sticking grotesquely above the surface. Others lay half in, half out of the water. Where the tails were in the water, they were dirty, matted and thin – an ignominious end to something that had been so fine and flowing and beautiful. But whether it was the heads or tails that were in the water, the teeth of all were bared in the grimace of death. And where the teeth were above the surface, beetles hunted where once they would have been the hunted.

Forcing herself forward, yet holding her head away from the stench of death, the little vixen tried to see if any of the bodies was that of the old fox. Some of them, she could see, were mature vixens whose coats had recovered from the summer strain of rearing cubs. There were also one or two fully-grown dogs, but most of them were young foxes cut down before they themselves could mate and bring others into the world. Such a waste, she thought, such a dreadful, dreadful waste. And for what?

At least, she thought, there was none among the young foxes that she knew. But what of the old fox? Fearing that he might lie where some were piled one upon the other, she continued to examine the line of corpses. Old, young, thin, fat, those who had hunted well and those who hadn't. Even two badgers, their long striped noses close to the fine brown nose of a fox in a way they would never have been in life. But none she knew, either young or old.

Relieved, but sickened by the sight and smell of death, the vixen stood staring at the terrible destruction until the bleating of sheep brought her out of her trance. Turning, she saw them watching her from the brow of a hill with that nervous curiosity sheep display when they see another animal that is not a sheep. At the same time, four grey crows landed close by, and theirs was no idle curiosity.

It wasn't the first time the little vixen had seen grey crows. She had often come across them as she trotted through the fields. But it was only now that she was face to face with them that she noticed each had a splash of black on its grey breast. It spread out across their breast like a great splayed claw, a jagged claw, which, combined with a swaggering walk, gave them not only a brash, but distinctly fearsome look.

As the vixen watched them strutting around, she realised that they were waiting for her to go, and slowly the awful truth seeped into her numbed mind that they had come, not to watch, but to feed upon the foxes. Giving vent to a cry of anguish, she tore into them, snapping and leaping, but in vain. With a slow, almost contemptuous flap of their wings, the crows lifted themselves off the ground only to land again a short distance away. There they walked around, unafraid, waiting like vultures to join the beetles and eat upon the eaters.

The wind had now turned cold. Like death itself, it would soon grip the countryside in an embrace that would stiffen the grass and turn the water to ice. As the little vixen fled across the fields, flocks of sheep scattered, then crowded together to watch her pass, but she was unaware of either their staring eyes or their frightened bleating. They had not the sense of know that they were watching one who was much more frightened than they. Only the rooks that flew a ragged path in the wind above knew her headlong flight across the fields was a sign of trouble.

The moon that night was big and bright and while it was still not full it covered the countryside in a soft yellow light which foxes know as gloomglow. Yet even that light could not pick out the little vixen as she lay and shivered in the ditch where she had taken refuge. Not that the comforting light would have given her any solace if it had. Having run to the point of exhaustion, she had collapsed in a state of shock beneath the branches of a guelder rose, and it was only the sensitive nose of another vixen that found her there next morning.

'Twinkle, Twinkle, is that you?'

The little vixen didn't answer, and the other licked the fur on her forehead clean to reveal a small white star.

'Twinkle, it *is* you. What happened?'

Through her half-closed eyes, the little vixen saw what she took to be her own tears glistening against the light of morning. Then, as she brought them into focus, they turned to red like drops of blood.

Startled, she made to run, but was restrained by her friend, who assured her. 'It's all right, Twinkle, it's only me.'

Realising that she had focused for a moment on the translucent red berries of the guelder rose, Twinkle sank back again, and whispered, 'Vickey. Thank goodness it's you.'

'What happened?' asked the other gently. 'How did you get into such a state?'

'The foxes, over on the bog, they're all dead . . . '

The one she had called Vickey sprang to her feet. 'Not Old Sage Brush?'

Twinkle shook her head. 'He wasn't among them. I don't know where he is.'

'And the others?'

'Young mostly, but,' she hastened to add, 'none that I knew.'

Vickey relaxed slightly. 'What happened to them?'

'Shot, all of them.' The little vixen lowered her head and cried. 'Oh Vickey, it was horrible. The beetles were crawling all over them, and the grey crows were waiting. I tried to drive them off, but I . . . I couldn't.'

'Don't. Don't distress yourself.' Vickey tried to comfort her, but she went on, 'They were just dumped there, but why, Vickey, why? Man didn't even want their fur. It was such a waste.'

Vickey shook her head. When hunting had been at its height they had suffered greatly at the hands of man. The choking hedge-traps had taken the biggest toll. Many foxes had been clubbed to death, others shot. She herself had come upon the awful sight of a fox that had been shot, skinned to the bone where it had fallen and left to rot. But why should man kill so many now and not even take their skins? And what were the implications for the rest of them?

'Come,' she said, 'I think the sooner we get under ground the better. We must talk, and we must warn the others. They too may be in danger.'

It was early in the morning, and man was still not about. Vickey led Twinkle up out of the ditch and across the fields of bleating sheep until they came to a long row of beeches. They trotted up a dry ditch beneath the trees, then cut across to a sprawling hedge of black-thorns. Deep in the blackthorns was an earth which, they knew, offered both comfort and safety.

For several seasons past, these same blackthorns had given protection to two other foxes who had also suffered at the hands of man. Their twisting branches, bristling as they were with the strongest and sharpest of thorns, had repelled many a trapper's hand, not to mention the soft paw of the fiercest dog.

'Hop-along,' Vickey called from the entrance.

A moment later, a three-legged fox hobbled up out of the earth, and seeing the distressed condition of one of his callers, immediately led them below. There he allowed Twinkle to settle into the warm den that he had just vacated.

Having related Twinkle's story to him, Vickey assured him that none of the young foxes was theirs. She began to groom the little vixen and lick some life back into her shivering body.

Hop-along lay down beside her. 'And she saw no sign of Old Sage Brush?'

Vickey looked at him and shook her head. 'She says his den in the birches was cold, but he wasn't among the dead.'

Just then Hop-along's mate arrived and he quickly told her what had happened.

'But why?' asked She-la. 'Why were they killed?'

Vickey shook her head. 'That's the puzzling thing about it.'

'They were just thrown there,' said Twinkle, who was now beginning to regain her composure. 'And I forgot to tell you,' She looked at Vickey; 'There were two badgers there as well.'

'Strange,' said Hop-along. He left them for a moment, and when he returned, he told them. 'No sign of any danger around Beech Paw.' He hobbled over to a corner and lay down, his nose resting where his leg should have been, and the others could see he was trying to assess the situation.

'This may mean great danger for all of us,' whispered She-la.

Vickey glanced at Hop-along, adding, 'And for some more than others.'

Twinkle struggled to her feet. 'What do you think we should do?'

Vickey considered for a moment. 'I think we should call a meeting.'

'You mean, under Beech Paw?' asked She-la.

Vickey nodded, and Hop-along, who had hobbled over to them, said, 'I agree. We may all be in great danger, and the more who know about it the better.'

'What's this meeting you're talking about?' asked Twinkle. 'What good will a meeting do?

Vickey lay down so as to put Twinkle more at ease, and when the young fox had settled herself again, she told her, 'We must alert as many other foxes as possible to what has happened, and the best way of doing that is to meet and talk about it.'

'You're too young to know,' said She-la, 'but always when great danger has threatened us, we have met under Beech Paw and decided what we should do about it. That is why we have survived here in the Land of Sinna when others have perished.'

Twinkle nodded. Young as she was, she had already come to know the circle of beeches at the top of the long row of trees as a place where she would meet her friends, and it had crossed her mind that there she soon might meet a mate.

'The last time we called a meeting under the beeches,' continued Vickey, 'was when the fur trappers were killing so many foxes we were afraid we might be wiped out.'

'That was before you were born,' Hop-along informed her.

'As a result of that meeting,' said Vickey, 'we went on a long journey. Hop-along, She-la, myself and others – and we learned how to survive. It was your grandfather who showed us – Old Sage Brush. Just the way he showed you and the other cubs how to cross the bog, remember?'

Twinkle nodded. How could she forget? Those days when the old fox had shown them the ways of the wild had been very happy ones. Vickey's own cubs, Young Black Tip and Little Running Fox had been there too. So had Hop-along and She-la's cubs, Scab and Scat. The old fox had taught them how to cross the bog with their eyes closed, and who better to show them? They had learned many other things from him too, things that had helped to keep them out of that heap of corpses now rotting over there on the edge of the bog where they had frolicked and played in the heat of summer.

'At least we might find out why they were killed,' said Hop-along. 'There must be a reason for it.'

Vickey smiled at him. 'You, above all foxes, should know man doesn't need a reason. You too She-la.'

She-la nodded, and seeing the questioning look on Twinkle's face, Vickey told her, 'She-la was shot once, down in the meadows. We didn't think she was going to survive.'

'But she did,' smiled Hop-along, 'and so did her cubs.'

'But why?' asked Twinkle.

'Man was building his dam down in the valley,' said Hop-along, 'and we were being a nuisance to him.'

She-la sighed: 'Just being a fox is reason enough.'

Hop-along nodded. 'Still, there must be some reason why he killed so many foxes at the one time and then just dumped them on the bog.'

Vickey knew there was great deal of truth in what She-la had said. Man never needed much reason to kill the fox. At the same time, she couldn't help thinking that She-la's view of man's action was clouded by what had happened to her. No, Hop-along was right. There had to be a reason, and the sooner they found out what it was, the better. Turning to Twinkle, she asked, 'How are you feeling now?'

Twinkle managed a smile. 'Much better.'

'Good. We'll need your help. Now, here's what we must do.'

TWO

Beyond the Bow

Man was asleep in the valley of Glensinna when the four foxes made their way to the circle of trees they called Beech Paw. Perhaps his dreams were troubled by foxes, those same foxes that had given their name to the valley long ago when Gaelic was the spoken tongue: Gleann an tSionnaigh Bháin, the Valley of the White Fox. There were some who said the foxes had brought the valley luck. However, man's attitude to his fellow creatures can change with circumstances, especially when there is money involved, and there were those who felt they could no longer afford the predations of the fox, or even the presence of the badger.

Had man seen the four foxes silhouetted against the moon, which was now round and full, his sleep would have been even more troubled, and had he known that they would soon be joined by others, he might not have slept at all.

Vickey looked up at the moon which they in the fox world knew as the wide eye of gloomglow, because it resembled the colour and shape of their own eyes, and wondered how many would answer their call. She herself had volunteered to search the bog in case Old Sage Brush might have returned, but all she found were the remains of those who would never hear the call of a vixen again. Moving beyond the bog, she had done what she had asked She-la and Twinkle to do before they had set out in different directions. Wherever foxes had been, or were likely to pass, she had left messages, informing them that a great tragedy had taken place, and asking them to come to the meeting at Beech Paw. The meeting, she told them, would take place when the wide eye of gloomglow next appeared in the night sky.

It was other vixens who answered the call first. As is the custom with foxes, some of the vixens had remained in the area at the end of the cubbing season, while most of the dogs had dispersed, the young to find territories of their own. The old and the handicapped had also stayed on in the territory they knew best, and they would come next. But what about Old Sage Brush? Would he come?

Vickey was just wondering how his daughter, Sinnéad, would react to the news of the corpses on the bog, when Sinnéad joined them. She touched noses with Twinkle, who was her daughter, and then turned to the others. Her questioning look told them she already knew the old fox was missing, and when some of them shook their heads, she lay down and looked up at the wide eye of gloomglow.

Vickey reckoned she was wondering if the same soft light was shining down on her aged father, out there, somewhere, or if the cold hand of death had descended on him too. Before she could say anything, another fox trotted in over the ring of earth that joined the roots of the beeches, and She-la went forward to greet him.

'It's Scab,' She-la exclaimed, recognising not only the scent but the mangy outline of one of her dog cubs. They rubbed noses, almost as if they hadn't seen each other for a long time and then joined Hop-along.

Vickey smiled. She knew, as indeed did the others, that there was hardly a night when Scab and his parents didn't meet, as he had stayed in the area because of his disability. Like Sinnéad, they were just glad to confirm that their offspring was still alive.

Others followed now – Ratwiddle, whose stiff neck and eccentric ways endeared himself to all, but whose fleas made them keep their distance; Skulking Dog, the mate of Sinnéad and the father of Twinkle; a stranger with no name and no tail . . .

So many were arriving now it was difficult to tell some of them apart. A handsome young dog fox approached Vickey, and she felt her heartbeat quicken. 'Black Tip?' she ventured, thinking for a moment it might be her mate.

'No,' he replied, and there was a twinkle in his eye. 'Young Black Tip.'

Overjoyed, Vickey greeted her dog cub warmly. 'And your father? Any news of him?'

Young Black Tip shook his head. 'The last time I saw him, I was running from the howling dogs. The two of us went into the river.' He paused. 'Only one of us came out.' Startled, Vickey took a step back. 'At least, I think he was there beside me,' Young Black Tip hastened to add. 'I'm not sure. I hardly knew what I was doing, or where I was. The howling dogs were breathing down my neck. I just thought he was there beside me, willing me on ... The next thing I knew, I was lying on a muddy bank half-drowned. Later I remember picking up his scent on the same side of the river and thinking he must have made it too.'

'Maybe then he's still alive,' said Vickey.

Young Black Tip diverted his eyes for a moment and when he looked at his mother again, he told her. 'I don't know. The scent seemed to go away into the woods, but then it came back to the river. I think maybe he went in again after the danger passed to look for me. But ... I can't be sure. Maybe he is still alive. I just don't know.'

Vickey lowered her head, then as if she was putting her fears for her mate to one side, or into some secret corner of her mind where she could retrieve them later on and think about them, she said, 'Old Sage Brush is missing too, you know.' She told Young Black Tip about Twinkle's gruesome find at the bog, and as she did so she couldn't help thinking that he had grown up to be a fine dog fox. Strong and handsome, she thought, just like his father.

When it appeared that all had come that were going to come, Vickey told them about the awful slaughter that had occurred. Some indicated that they were already aware of it, while those who didn't know of it got up and spoke to each other in a way that clearly showed their alarm, and asked Twinkle to tell them more.

'Furthermore,' said Vickey when Twinkle had finished. 'Old Sage Brush has gone missing.'

This news spread even greater alarm through the assembled foxes, for the old fox was known far and wide for the wisdom that enabled him to survive, even though he was blind.

'We've looked everywhere,' Vickey continued, 'but there's no sign of him.'

'Perhaps you didn't look hard enough,' whispered a voice beside her.

'Old Sage Brush?' Vickey jumped to her feet.

Sinnéad and Twinkle rushed over to rub noses with the old fox, and Twinkle said, 'We thought you were dead.'

Old Sage Brush smiled. 'It's hard to get rid of a bad thing.'

'We didn't hear you coming in,' said Vickey.

Old Sage Brush chuckled. He enjoyed coming upon his fellow foxes unawares. 'Sometimes,' he told her, 'when we listen to one thing, we do not hear another.'

Realising the significance of what the old fox was saying, Vickey immediately asked some of the other foxes to position themselves o the rim of earth between the beeches. There they could keep one ear on what was being said and the other on the surrounding coun- tryside so that they wouldn't be caught off guard.

'You told me once the bog was like a spider's web,' said Twinkle. 'I thought perhaps you had been caught in it.'

'It is like a spider's web' replied the old fox. 'But we aren't like spiders. We don't have to hang around, hoping that man won't see us especially when there is a strong smell of death in the air.'

'You were right to go. I saw the bodies of many foxes. Man just dumped them at the edge of the bog.'

'Why do you think man should shoot so many of our kind?' asked a fox from within the circle.

'They were not all shot,' said Vickey. 'Some had fallen victim to the choking hedge-trap.'

'But I thought the young fox said ...'

'I know what she said,' Vickey went on. 'She was upset.'

'And some were piled on top of one another,' explained Twinkle. 'It was difficult to see ...'

'What's important,' said another, 'is not how they died but why.'

Old Sage Brush agreed. 'We know from past experience that man has used our fur to keep himself warm. But if these foxes were dumped, it means they weren't killed for their fur.'

'And it was hardly because they were taking man's chickens,' reasoned Skulking Dog.

'Why not?' asked another.

'Because there were badgers there too, and badgers don't hunt chickens.'

'Man, in his ignorance, does many things,' said Old Sage Brush. 'How are we to know what was in his mind when death was in his hands?'

'I know the answer to the question you are all asking.' said a fox who had just arrived. 'They were killed because they were in Sheep Land.'

'All land is now Sheep Land as far as I can see,' Sinnéad remarked.

'True,' said the other fox, 'but in the land I speak of, the sheep had just begun to have their lambs. The grey crows pecked some of the lambs to death, and then the farmer found one with its head chopped off, so he ...'

'He blamed the fox,' continued Old Sage Brush. 'All those foxes for just one lamb.' He sighed. 'When will man ever learn that most of us don't like lamb?'

'I prefer rabbits,' said another.

A murmur of 'Don't we all' ran through the assembled foxes.

'But there are some of us who got a taste for lamb when the sleeping sickness killed off the rabbits,' said another. 'And it's hard to pass it by when the opportunity arises.'

'If man loses a lamb it's his own fault,' said a voice from the back. 'He should keep them in until they're big enough.'

'It's not as if he hasn't enough sheep,' said another. 'The land is full of them. I've never seen so many in all my life.'

'And there will be more,' Old Sage Brush reminded them. 'I'm told the grey crows are gathering. That means lambing time will be upon the Land of Sinna very shortly, and then we will all be in danger.'

As the foxes turned to consult each other and consider their predicament, one of those who had been keeping an ear to the surrounding countryside warned them to be quiet. Some rose to their feet, ready to run.

'It's all right,' said the fox who had given the warning, 'it's only badgers.'

Moments later a badger boar and a sow scrambled on to the embankment and slithered rather clumsily down into the middle of the foxes. The nearest ones jumped back, then rounded on the badgers for interrupting their meeting.

Vickey ran over. 'Take it easy. Can't you see they're running, not feeding?'

The badgers were out of breath, and seeing that they posed no danger, the foxes gathered around.

'You sound as if you are in trouble?' said Old Sage Brush gently.

The sow lifted her long snout and looked at him with her tiny eyes. 'We have been travelling for many nights. Running, feeding, trying to keep on the move.'

'What are you running from?' asked Sinnéad.

The boar had now recovered his breath. 'We come from the Land of the Cow,' he told her. 'Our setts have been destroyed, many of our kind wiped out.'

The sow laid her slender head on her powerful claws and moaned.

'The cubs of our last litter,' said the boar. 'All gone. Young, old, it made no difference. Man killed them all.'

'We were out feeding,' the sow continued. 'When we came back it was all over.'

'But why?' asked Twinkle. 'Surely man doesn't think you kill his sheep.'

The boar shook his head. 'There are very few sheep where we come from.'

''Perhaps he thinks we are unclean,' said the sow.

'How could he think that?' consoled Vickey. 'He must know the way you groom yourselves and air your bedding.'

'That is true,' said the sow, 'but in spite of everything we sometimes have sickness.'

'I think we get it from the cows when they come nosing around us in the fields at night,' added the boar.

'Maybe man thinks his cows get the sickness from you,' suggested Old Sage Brush.

'The way his cows are always slobbering over each other, I think they get it from each other,' said the sow.

'Whatever the truth of it,' continued the old fox, 'the fact remains that you are in a predicament, just as we are.' He told them about the corpses of the foxes and badgers that Twinkle had found on the bog, adding. 'The question is, what are we going to do about it?'

'What can we do?' asked the boar. 'We can run, but not very fast. We can see, but not very well.'

'One who cannot see very well can see much better than one who cannot see at all,' said the old fox. 'And the eyes of the dead who lie upon the bog, must open the eyes of those who live.'

Hop-along hobbled over to renew his acquaintance with Old Sage Brush, and they went aside for a quiet talk.

'Your friend speaks in strange ways,' the boar badger remarked. 'I find it difficult to follow his meaning.'

Vickey nodded. 'I suppose it is difficult for those who do not know him. But once he has opened your eyes, it is easier to see his meaning.'

The badger looked at his mate, as if to say, 'This fox is talking in riddles too,' but before they could say anything more, one of the foxes on look-out warned that something else was coming.

They all cocked their ears.

'Another badger,' whispered one fox.

'. . . Not a badger,' said Old Sage Brush. 'If I'm not mistaken that's . . . an otter.'

A shadowy figure appeared on the rim of earth between the trees, and stood up to present a familiar outline against the moonlit sky.

Vickey smiled. She had never known the old fox's sense of hearing to fail him. 'You're right. It is an otter.'

Their latest visitor scrambled down the slope and made its way over to them. 'Why, it's Whiskers!' exclaimed Vickey and, rushing forward, greeted the otter as warmly as she had greeted any of her own kind.

Having acknowledged Old Sage Brush, Hop-along and others among them that he knew, the otter looked at Young Black Tip, who was standing close to Vickey. 'And who is this?'

'Don't you remember?' she asked him. 'Don't you remember the cub the hunting bird dropped in the lake? The one who would have drowned, but for you?'

'Ah,' said Whiskers. 'The little fox with the black tip on his tail. Do you know, he's the water-image of his father. And speaking of his father. I don't see him?'

Vickey lowered her head. 'No. We were hoping he would come if he was still . . . '. She sighed. 'But we're afraid he may not be.'

Realising that Vickey couldn't bring herself to say she was afraid he might not be still alive, Whiskers said,

'From what I remember, your good friend Black Tip was a strong fox, just like his offspring here. Don't worry, he's well able to look after himself.'

'That's what I've been trying to tell her,' said Old Sage Brush, who was lying nearby.

She-la looked at Vickey in a way that offered her consolation, saying, 'He'll come. He must. We need all the strength we can get.'

'Why, what's the problem?' inquired Whiskers.

Sinnéad, who was now standing beside her father, told the otter how the old fox had had to flee from his home in the bog when man had dumped a terrible death upon it. 'We think man may have done it to protect his lambs,' she added. 'And some of us fear we may be next.'

'Man also brings death to our homes,' Whiskers told them. 'His dogs chase us, just as they chase you. Our cubs get caught in his long eel nets and drown. But it is what he dumps in the water that is the worst.'

'What could be worse than being chased and killed?' asked Twinkle.

'That's right,' said her father, Skulking Dog. He had out-run many a pack of howling dogs, and felt the sting of man's pellets upon his rump.

'Man kills in many ways,' the old fox reminded them. 'Let the otter continue.'

'It's his poisons that are the worst,' Whiskers went on, 'for we find them everywhere. In the streams, the ditches, the rivers: anything he doesn't want he dumps into the water. It's as if he thinks it's out of the way when it's out of sight. But it's not. When the water

22

becomes dead, so does everything in it, and then we have no food. The fish float with their bellies to the sky, but we cannot eat them or we too will get sick and die. Even the heron loses its patience and takes to the sky. But just as you are bound to the earth, so we are bound to the water. We have to live there, and we cannot do that unless it provides us with food.'

'So what are you going to do?' asked Vickey. 'Where are you going? I mean, I take it you haven't answered our call to come to this meeting?'

Whiskers shook his head. 'No, no.' He raised himself on his hind legs and leaned back upon his tail so that he remained upright, and told them, 'Today, before darkness came upon the valley, and rain fell upon the water, I saw a sign.'

He paused and a murmur ran through the foxes as they wondered what it was.

'It was the sign,' he told them, 'that we in the otter world call the Great Bow. It filled the sky with many colours and it filled my mind with wondrous things – things I have seen, and must see again, things I have done and must do again, places I have been, and must go to again . . .'

Many of the foxes gathered under the beeches had also seen the Bow in the Cloud, and if, as seems likely, man had lifted his eyes from his sheep to glance at it, he would have described its colours as red, orange, yellow, green, blue, indigo and violet.

'I know when I saw it,' Whiskers continued, 'that I must be on my way again, leave all this filth that man has dumped in the rivers, and go to a place where he himself is but a leaf cast upon the water.'

The foxes and the badgers had all gathered round now and were listening, spellbound, to what the otter was telling them.

'Where is this place you speak of? asked Old Sage Brush. 'This place where man, not us, might be at the mercy of the elements?'

'Beyond the Great Bow,' Whiskers told him. 'Beyond the hills, where it comes to rest.'

'And where is that?' asked the sow badger.

Knowing that because of their poor eyesight, and the fact that they seldom if ever came out during the day, badgers would never even have seen the Bow in the Cloud, Whiskers replied, 'How can one who has never seen such a glorious sign, one who seldom ventures beyond her own field, possibly imagine where the Great Bow might end?'

'When I had a tail,' said the fox with none, 'I used to chase it. But it was a chase with no end. Somehow I always felt the Great Bow was the same.'

'Well said,' commented the old fox, and taking a deep breath he expelled it in such a way that the others could see he was weighing up what the otter had told them.

'But when I go on my travels,' said Whiskers, 'I don't go round in circles.'

'And this place you speak so warmly of? asked She-la. 'I know you said it was at the end of the Great Bow. But where exactly is it?'

'It's at the Edge of the World,' Whiskers told them.

An uncomfortable murmur went through the assembled foxes, some of them saying, 'The Edge of the World? Did you hear what he said? The Edge of the World.'

'Of course,' Whiskers went on. 'You don't think the world goes on forever, do you?'

Needless to say, this was all beyond the comprehension of those who had never been much farther than their own territories, and one of the foxes asked, 'But what's it like?'

Whiskers eased himself down on all fours. 'What's it like?' He rolled over, and lying on his back the way he would float upon the water, looked up at the night sky.

The foxes at the back crowded closer, craning their necks to see what he was doing and hear what he had to say.

'Well,' Whiskers began, 'it's like nothing any one of you has ever seen. The water is as blue as the sky, and stretches farther than the eye can see. The fish are so plentiful I hardly know which to catch, and when I tire of eating, I chase them for fun. When I tire of playing, well, I just turn over on my back and float. The water rocks me to sleep, and then I dream.'

THREE

Flowers of the Field

'I have dreams too,' said Ratwiddle. Because of his stiff neck, his head was cocked to one side so that he also was looking at the sky.

Some of the younger foxes giggled, and said, 'What have you dreamed, Ratwiddle? Tell us. What have you dreamed?'

Whether Ratwiddle knew the young were making fun of him, who could tell? But he replied, 'I have seen man walk upon the water as he hunts for fish. I have seen a great green caterpillar hunting for man in the sky. And I've seen the rats. The rats . . . ' His voice trailed off. 'I've seen the rats hunting the fox.'

The young foxes, and even some older ones who did not know him, laughed.

'You can laugh if you like,' said Ratwiddle, 'but these things I have seen in the darkness of my mind.' So saying, he got up and going over the gnarled roots of one of the beech trees, lay down and began to scratch himself vigorously.

The young foxes continued to giggle, and Old Sage Brush rebuked them. 'Laugh not at what you do not understand,' he told them. 'Ratwiddle has hunted the rats, but he in turn has been hunted by them, and now the sickness is lodged in his mind like the seed in the belly of a jennet.'

The young foxes hung their heads, realising, as indeed they were meant to, that not only had they been unkind, but, because they did not understand, there were short-comings in their own minds.

'Sorry,' mumbled one of them.

The old fox grunted, as if to say, 'So you should be.'

He walked over to where Sinnéad and Skulking Dog, Hop-along and She-la were, and when he was out of ear-shot, Young Black Tip whispered to his mother, 'What's a jennet?'

The other young foxes crowded around as they too wanted to know.

Now man might say that foxes wouldn't know about such a thing as a jennet, but then what animal knows more about its fellow creatures than a fox, and who can say what it sees as it traverses the fields by day and night? All man can say with certainty is that many of his own kind do not know what a jennet is because they know little of the fields.

'A jennet,' Vickey replied, 'is neither a horse nor a donkey. It is the offspring of both, but it is also barren and cannot have offspring of its own. In the same way, Ratwiddle is neither sensible nor silly. His mind cannot produce thoughts in the same way that you and I can, but he has a strange way of knowing things. Things that have not yet happened.'

'How can he do that?' asked the fox with no tail who had also heard what she had said.

'Who can tell? But before man ever built his dam in this valley, Ratwiddle saw the water rising.'

Old Sage Brush came back over to them and lay down beside Vickey. 'I have been talking to Hop-along and his friends. It is the dreams of the otter that we want to hear about. Is he still here?'

Whiskers was talking to the badgers, to which he and his kind were distantly related.

'You say that when you float upon the water, you dream,' said Old Sage Brush. 'What do you dream about?'

Whiskers came over and, lying down, rested his whiskered snout on his forepaws. He sighed as if recalling a great contentment, and they knew he was savouring the memories of those wonderful moments he had spent at the Edge of the World.

'I dream of many pleasures,' he told them. 'The pleasure of hunting in water that is as pure as it is blue, the pleasure of watching the birds diving for food and knowing there is plenty for everyone; the pleasure of swimming where there are no traps; the pleasure – oh the indescribable pleasure – of closing my eyes and knowing man will not creep up on me.'

'You mean man is not to be found there?' asked Hop-along.

'Oh, he's there all right,' said Whiskers. 'But he is not a hunting man. It's almost as if the water is too vast for him, almost as if he is afraid of it.' Whiskers opened his eyes. 'Do you know that when he is fishing at the edge and the water comes in, he runs away from it!'

The others laughed, and Sinnéad said, 'But I thought you said he didn't hunt?'

'Neither he does,' Whiskers replied, 'except for fish, that is. Do you know I sometimes think he's even afraid of otters. It's as if he was seeing some strange creature and didn't know what it was.'

'What about badgers?' asked the sow. 'Does he hunt them?'

Whiskers shook his head. 'On the contrary. I have heard that he sometimes feeds them.'

A murmur of disbelief ran through the crowd.

'And what about foxes?' asked Hop-along's cub, Scab. 'I'm sure he doesn't feed them.'

'Maybe not,' said Whiskers, 'but them again I've never seen him hunt them there either.'

'I've seen man feed a fox here in the Land of Sinna.' Skulking Dog told them.

'That's right,' said Vickey. 'His name was Needle Nine.'

'When his parents were killed by the trappers,' Skulking Dog continued, 'man reared him on the farm down by the lake.'

'There were sheep on that farm too,' Vickey recalled, 'but man didn't seem to worry about having Needle Nine around. I wonder what became of him?'

No one knew, and when there was no answer Old Sage Brush resumed the conversation about he Edge of the World. 'And what about food?' he asked Whiskers. 'I mean, food for foxes.'

'The sky at the Edge of the World is teeming with birds,' the otter told him. 'But, better still, the hills are full of rabbits. They burrow in sand that is soft. They are not sick and they multiply quickly. Man does not seem to hunt them either. Somehow I think he has developed other pleasures, for he seems to spend his time walking and talking with his own kind, hitting stones with sticks and hunting for them in the long grass, No, he's too busy with his own pleasures to be bothered with us.'

Whiskers rolled over and lay on his back again. 'As for me, I dream of my pleasures. The pleasure of freedom and the pleasure of my own kind. There are other otters there, you know, male . . . and female. We romp and play to our heart's content, and when I find a female that enjoys my company, that is the greatest pleasure of all.'

The otter's story contained many things that were not within the experience or understanding of either the foxes or badgers, and the circle of beeches was filled with silence as they thought about some of the things he had told them.

After a few moments, the silence was broken by an unbelieving grunt from Skulking Dog. 'Sounds too good to be true,' he said. Others nodded. 'And these birds you speak of. Are there any chickens among them?'

'Whiskers shook his head. 'No. But a bird's a bird. They all have two legs.'

'Are there any flowers there?' asked the fox with no tail.

The others thought that was a strange question to ask, but waited for the reply.

'Some,' said Whiskers, 'Why?'

The tail–less fox shrugged. 'It's just that I sometimes think we are like the flowers in the fields. They must be there for a purpose. Yet man has no use for them. He looks upon them as weeds and destroys them.'

Vickey looked at the fox, impressed by the manner in which he had thought of their predicament, and Old Sage Brush nodded.

Others, however, were not so impressed.

'Such sentiments are all very fine,' said one, 'but what are we going to do?'

'Just one more thing,' Old Sage Brush said to Whiskers. 'Are there any sheep at the Edge of the World?'

Whiskers thought for a moment. 'I have never seen them there.'

'I agree with my friend,' said another fox. 'This is all very fine, but with due respect to the otter – and I thank him for lifting our hearts at this time of crisis – the problem is here and now, and the answer is not to be found in some far distant place that may . . . ' He glanced at Whiskers, 'that may, or may not exist.'

In his own mind Whiskers could still see himself floating on a full stomach on the gentle rise and fall of the vast expanse of water on the Edge of the World, and the words of the fox went sailing over his head like one of the many great white birds he would see there.

'For you who are strong,' Old Sage Brush told the other fox, 'it is enough that you should know why so many of our kind lie lifeless on the bog. The problem is for us who are weak . . . Ratwiddle there, who lives by wits he does not have, Hop-along, who chewed off his paw so that he could run from man, Scab who faced the flame in the field to burn the itch from his back, the badger who flees from man though he can barely see, and I, an old fox, who cannot see at all.'

While Old Sage Brush's blindness was well known in the fox world, it was news to the badgers, and only now did they understand what he had meant when he had said that those with poor sight could see better than those who could not see at all.

Twinkle reached up to nudge her grandfather with her nose, and the old fox acknowledged her gesture of affection.

'The problems of others,' said a voice from the back, 'are not our problems.' There was an uncomfortable pause, and the voice added, 'I mean . . . Well, I don't mean other foxes.'

'I know what you mean,' said the old fox. 'And I know that the problems of others are sometimes our opportunity. But the badger is not our enemy. He sometimes allows us to share his sett, yet he does not ask us to share our food. So has he not a right to seek our help?'

'But how can we help them?' asked another fox. 'How can we even help our own?'

'I am not suggesting that you should,' said the old fox. 'What I am saying is that perhaps the weak may find strength in each other.'

'How can that be,' asked the other fox, 'when even the strong may not be able to help the weak?'

'You must not forget,' said Old Sage Brush, 'that we also have inner strengths, and anyway, it depends on what we want to do – where we want to go.'

'And where are you going?' asked the fox with no tail.

Old Sage Brush turned his sightless eyes towards the sky.

'I have lived for many seasons,' he replied. 'I have travelled far and wide. I know the pathways of the bog like a spider knows its own web. But after listening to our friend the otter, I feel my world has become quite small, and suddenly I have this great urge to go to the Edge of the World.'

The otter rolled back on to his feet and sat up with a start, the badgers squinted at the old fox to see if he was serious, the strangers among the foxes looked at him as if they thought he had gone mad, while Vickey and her friends looked at each other, as if they couldn't believe their own ears.

Old Sage Brush chuckled. 'No need to be concerned,' he told them. 'I haven't taken leave of my senses. At least, not yet. Now, you among us who are healthy and well, may I suggest you be on your way before daylight finds you here. My advice is that you learn well from what you have heard. Stay away from man's sheep and perhaps he will stay away from you.'

Most of the foxes turned, and with a flick of their fine bushy tails, were gone.

'Sage Brush,' said Vickey gently.

'I know, I know. You are going to tell me that I am too old for such foolishness, that I would not be able for such a journey.' Her silence and the silence of the others told him he had read her mind correctly. 'But don't forget, we've had a sign. The otter said so.'

Some nodded. As cubs, their parents had told them a story from foxlore about the Bow in the Cloud. Wherever they saw it, their parents had assured them, they would know it was a sign that whatever happened, the creatures of the earth would somehow survive.

'But you have also told us,' said Skulking Dog, 'that according to foxlore it is here in the Land of Sinna that the fox will survive, just as we survived when man flooded the valley.'

'That is true,' said the old fox, 'but it is also true and perhaps more important, that it is here we have learned how to survive. What happens when the lambs come to the Land of Sinna? Where will I find the strength to run then? Where will Hop-along find another leg?'

'And where will I find the brush that will give me the balance I need to turn quickly from danger?' asked the other voice.

'Ah, the stranger with no tail.' Old Sage Brush smiled. 'Somehow I find it difficult to imagine a fox with no tail. And aren't you the one who spoke of the flowers of the field?'

When the other confirmed that he was the one, the old fox went on, 'Well, you may not be able to turn your body as quickly as you would wish, but I must say I like your turn of mind. Come forward so that I can see you. Without a tail you must look like one of those small dogs man uses when he digs us out for fun.'

'He looks sort of . . . well, stumpy,' ventured Vickey, not wishing to offend the other fox. 'You don't mind if I call you Stumpy, do you?'

'When you are happy to be alive, you are happy to have a name – any name,' he replied.

'And was it the fun dogs who deprived you of your tail?' asked Old Sage Brush.

'No. It was the howling dogs. Or at least, it was their masters. But tell me old fox, how can you see me if you are blind?'

'When you look into your own mind, you can see many things – even things that are in the minds of others.'

'But Sage Brush,' said Sinnéad, 'how can you go on such a journey? And even if you could go, who would go with you?'

'Those who must go, will go. Hop-along, Ratwiddle, our friends the badgers, and perhaps some who are strong.'

Ratwiddle got up. Without a word, he hopped up on to the rim of earth that linked the beeches and disappeared into the night.

On being told who had gone, the old fox said. 'Don't worry, he'll be all right. I forgot, it is not his body that is weak, but his mind.'

'If you really feel you must go to the Edge of the World,' said Skulking Dog, 'I will go with you.'

'And so will I,' said Young Black Tip.

Feeling his grand-daughter, Twinkle, quiver beside him, and knowing she was going to offer to go too, Old Sage Brush shook his head. 'I thank you, Young Black Tip, but no. You are entering upon your first season as a mature fox, and no one has the right to deprive you of that. So is Twinkle here, and Little Running Fox, and all those other young foxes who have survived the summer. Skulking Dog will come with us. . . . And Sinnéad. And perhaps you too, Vickey?'

Vickey smiled. 'Of course. Once Black Tip was our eyes, and since he is no longer with us, the least I can do is take his place.'

'And what about the badgers?' said the old fox. 'I take it you are coming with us?'

The boar badger raised his long snout in the air, and began, 'Well . . . I . . . '

The sow sniffed, and said quickly, 'Yes we are. We're coming too.'

'Good,' said Vickey. 'And what shall we call you?'

'My name's Sniff,' replied the sow.

'And I'm Snout,' said her mate.

'You realise we will have to travel by day?' said Old Sage Brush.

'By day?' repeated the boar badger. 'But it's not in our nature to move around by day.'

'You might think it's not in the nature of ants to fly,' said the old fox. 'Yet, I have seen them sprout wings and take to the air. When the lambs come, many dangers will await us, and we must be able to rise above them.'

'But if we travel by day,' Hop-along reminded him, 'we will not have the Great Running Fox to guide us.'

Seeing that the badgers were puzzled, She-la pointed with her nose to the cluster of stars which man calls the Plough.

'That is the Great Running Fox in the Sky, the one my mate speaks of,' she told them. 'It guides us on our nightly travels. But Hop-along is right.' She turned Old Sage Brush. 'Who will guide us by day?'

'Who else?' replied the old fox, 'but the otter.'

'That's right,' said Whiskers triumphantly. 'You follow me.'

'And who will guide you?' asked Vickey.

Whiskers smiled. 'No one. I just follow the river.'

FOUR

Like Ducks in Thunder

The hills were dark and misty. Grey rain clouds covered the valley to which Whiskers had now brought his friends, and wherever there was a possibility of food, birds watched the farms and waited.

Having left the Land of Sinna to the strong, and the sheep fields to the grey crows, foxes and badgers had followed Whiskers across country in the early dawn until they had come to a stream.

'Is this the one that will lead us to the Edge of the World?' asked Old Sage Brush.

'I'm not sure yet,' Whiskers replied. 'It will take me a little time to get my bearings.'

For reasons best known to himself, Whiskers had decided that the river that ran from the Land of Sinna was not the one they should follow, and had sought out a stream in the hills.

From a peaty and often frothy beginning, this stream had cut a path for itself so that it flowed between rocks and deep earthen gullies, slowly widening as it picked its way down into the gently sloping valley. Sheep that grazed near its higher reaches raised their heads to watch with great curiosity as first the otter, then the badgers, and finally the foxes, made their way among the clumps of heather.

Scots pine, and further down, other evergreens and beeches told them they were nearing the haunts of man. Beyond the beeches, they found themselves in brown rushy meadows where trenches formed by man's efforts to drain the land gave them plenty of cover. Gradually the river became wide and shallow. Sometimes it would split, flow around a low pebbly bank and then become one again. Occasionally it would bubble over a stony patch and there it would gurgle as if in celebration of its arrival among green fields that sustained more life.

Whiskers was nipping in and out of the river, sniffing its scents and exploring its banks. Sometimes he would sit back on his tail and look ahead. Then it was into the river again, swimming under the surface where it was deep enough, scurrying over the pebbles where it wasn't. And when, as often happened, Snout and Sniff stopped to rest he would go ahead, searching for food and confirming, or so the others hoped, that he had found the right river.

In the muddier meadows, the sheep looked dirty and bedraggled, but up on the hillsides, the foxes noticed they looked much cleaner and whiter.

'Tell me what you see,' said Old Sage Brush.

They were lying in the undergrowth at the edge of a plantation of evergreens, not far from the river.

'Up on the hill,' Vickey told him, 'on the other side of the river, I see man and a sheep-dog.'

'Any grey crows?'

'One or two flying over, But no. Mostly rooks . And some gulls. They're watching man putting out hay for the sheep.'

'I wish someone would feed us,' said Scab.

'You're a big cub now,' said She-la. 'You're well able to look after yourself.'

'Anyway Scab,' said the old fox, 'you wouldn't like hay. Take my word for it.'

Scab smiled. 'It wasn't hay I was thinking of.'

'So you've heard the ducks too?' The old fox turned to Vickey. 'Why didn't you mention them?'

'You asked me to tell you what I could see, not what I could hear.' Vickey paused. 'Anyway, I didn't want to upset you. What's the use of talking about something we can't have.'

Old Sage Brush didn't answer right away and when he did, he said, 'Just because we don't want lamb, doesn't mean we can't have ducks – or their eggs.'

Sinnéad stepped forward. 'But it's too dangerous. Sheep mean trouble. Why else did we have to leave the Land of Sinna?'

'Still,' said the old fox, 'the fact that we have to run from sheep, doesn't mean we have to act like them. And it is a long time since I've had a taste of duck.'

Sinnéad looked at Skulking Dog in a way that clearly said she thought her father was getting very contrary in his old age, but her mate didn't react in a way that gave her any support. He himself had always been very fond of farmyard fowl. Personally he preferred chickens, but he wouldn't say no to a duck.

Moving over to Old Sage Brush, he said, 'Would you like me to go and have a look?'

'Why not?' said the old fox. 'But not now. Wait until it's nearly dark – bright enough for you to see any choking hedge-traps that man might have left out for us, but dark enough to give you cover.'

'There are dogs up there,' warned Sinnéad. 'You heard what Vickey told you. What happens if you bring them down upon us?'

Old Sage Brush sighed. 'The dogs are guarding the sheep. You are guarding us. So what is there to worry about?'

Sinnéad felt the old fox was being deliberately mischievous. He sometimes got like that, mischievous and stubborn. It was a mood she had seen him in before. She looked at Hop-along and then at his mate. She-la, she could see, was just as worried as she was.

Sensing their concern, Sage Brush said, 'I just feel like a change, that's all.' Snout and Sniff were snuffling around for food of their own, and hearing them, he smiled and added, 'Worms may satisfy the needs of the badger but hardly the whim of a wily old fox. Now, it may be some time before we can figure out what we're going to do. Until then, we'll have to settle for something else. So don't just stand there like ducks in thunder. See what you can find.'

'Sage Brush,' said Vckey when the others had gone, 'You're in a funny mood.'

The old fox chuckled. 'Why do you say that?'

'You know why. First you tell us to stay sway from

41

sheep farms, and then you tell Skulking Dog to go there and hunt.'

'I didn't tell you to stay away from sheep farms,' the old fox reminded her. 'I told you to stay away from the sheep. And that doesn't' mean you must stop being a fox.'

Vickey shook her head. She knew exactly how Sinnéad must have felt, so she decided to change the subject. Sniff and Snout had now burrowed their way into the undergrowth and she could hear them snoring. 'Do you think they'll be able to make it?' she asked.

'I don't know. It depends on how far they want to go. Perhaps they'll come across a family of badgers that will take them in.'

'And how about you?'

The old fox shrugged. 'In some ways, I suppose I am like the river. As it gets older and wiser it travels more slowly. But it also gathers strength along the way.'

Vickey knew that while this was true of the river, it wasn't necessarily true of him. 'Sinnéad's not worried for her own sake, you know. She's worried that you might draw trouble upon yourself, and upon Hop-along. So am I.'

'I know that, but there's no need to worry,' the old fox assured her. 'At least, not yet. If the lambs arrive on the farm, the grey crows will tell us. Then it will be time to worry.'

Whiskers was anxious to be on his way, but he could see the badgers were tired, and Old Sage Brush was adamant. Personally, he couldn't imagine how the foxes were going to get at the ducks without drawing danger upon themselves. The situation held no danger for him;

he could be into the river and away before the sheep-dogs even knew he was there. It was just that he was in a hurry. Or was he? As he thought about it, he realised there was always the possibility that the foxes might succeed. In that event there would be plenty of food to go round, a type of food he hadn't had for a long time. Duck eggs, he recalled, had quite a strong tang, a tang that he liked ... Perhaps, on reflection, he wasn't in so much of a hurry after all.

'That settles it then,' said the old fox. 'Time to see what we can do.'

It was agreed that while Skulking Dog would go in and survey the situation, Stumpy would wait at the lower fence on the far side of the river to give him any assistance he needed. It seemed, however, that their plan was doomed to failure before it even started. On crossing the river, they found that the sheep wire was of such a small mesh they couldn't squeeze through. Furthermore, as they trotted up along it, they found that a sheep had put its black head through the fence and was bawling to tell all and sundry that it was trapped.

'It's only a matter of time before the farmer comes down to free it,' said Skulking Dog when they reported back.

'Where exactly is it?' asked Old Sage Brush.

'A hedge runs up to the farmyard.' Stumpy told him. 'On one side of that, just down the river a bit, its the field we tried to get into first.'

'On the other side are the fields that lead up to the paddock where the ewes are waiting to have their lambs,' said Skulking Dog. 'It's in the fence at the bottom of those fields that the sheep is trapped. It's just a short distance up the river.'

'If only I could get through the fence,' said Stumpy, 'I might have some chance.'

'In what way?' asked Hop-along.

'Well, they'd have to be a tails length nearer me to catch me?'

The others laughed.

'Unfortunately,' he added, 'I can't get through the fence either.'

'We could try,' said She-la. 'We're smaller.'

Skulking Dog shook his head. 'Not small enough.'

'I could get through,' said Scab. 'I'm thin and I've very little fur.'

Hop-along and She-la looked up in alarm.

'What do you think?' asked the old fox.

Skulking Dog nodded. 'I think he could.'

'But that would be putting him in needless danger protested his mother.

'Danger, perhaps, She-la,' replied the old fox. 'But not needless.'

'Old Sage Brush is right,' Hop-along told his mate. 'Scab led a very sheltered life back in the Land of Sinna. Maybe it's time he went out into the real world.'

'Don't worry,' Scab assured them. 'I'll be all right. After all, I had a good teacher.'

She-la smiled. 'I know. Sage Brush has taught you well.' She sighted. 'All right. So be it.'

The light was beginning to fade as Skulking Dog led Scab across the river by way of a shallow patch, and down along the fence to the place where he had tried to get through. Scab put his front legs in over the lower strand of one of the small wire squares, lowered his ears and squeezed forward until his paws were touching the ground. A bit more pushing and pulling, and soon the rest of his body was through too. Skulking Dog assured him that he would be there if he needed him, and with a last glance back, he ran quickly up along the hedge towards the farmhouses. At the end of the hedge, he found a clump of scrub that included elderberry, and from there he looked at the nearest shed. The tracks of the ducks, he could see, led into a hole at the bottom of the shed where a concrete block had been removed. Quickly he ran over and nipped in through the hole.

Inside, Scab found that a small corner of the shed had been railed off with wooden pallets to form a pen for the ducks. There was a strong smell of them in the straw on the floor, and hoping they might be brought in soon, he hopped up on the edge of the pen. Several other larger pens, he could see, contained a number of ewes and newborn lambs, and there was an even stronger smell of something man was using on them. It was an unpleasant smell, but then all of the smells he associated with man were unpleasant. Lights hung from the roof and fearing he might be seen, he made his way across to where bales of hay were stacked, clambered up them and hid in a dark recess at the top.

A short time later he saw the ducks waddling in through the hole in the wall, but his hopes of grabbing one and running off with it were dashed when something was placed against the hole from the outside. The ducks, he realised, had been closed in for the night – and so had he!

During the night Scab watched and waited. He knew he could kill all the ducks if he wanted to. But he also knew he would be killed himself once the racket started and he was discovered. He could smell the scent of a cat that had been up on the bales earlier in the day, but thankfully it was no longer around. Several times he shrank back into the shadows when the door opened and man came in to check the lambs. More than once he considered making a run for it through the open door. Then he thought of the ducks, and decided to wait.

Hanging from one of the walls were several sheepskins which the farmer had cured, and Scab wondered if this was the reason man reared so many sheep. His parents had told him that once they had seen man wearing a coat made from fox furs and knowing how mangy his own coat was, he had to suppress a laugh.

At long last the door was opened and left open. Still Scab didn't stir. Someone was moving about the yard and from somewhere in the distance there was the bark of a dog. Down below him, the ducks were getting noisy and restless now. Suddenly the covering was taken from the hole, and the ducks waddled out into the daylight.

Seizing his chance, Scab sped down across the bales and hopped over into the pen. Nosing around in the hay that covered the floor, he discovered, to his delight, that the ducks had laid a number of eggs. Taking one in his mouth, he peeped out around the edge of the hole. There was no one to be seen, so he dashed across to the clump of scrub and hid it in withered grass. He could tell from the sounds on the other side of the shed that man was busy with the sheep and new-born lambs. Quickly he ran back and forth to the duck pen until he had removed all of the eggs. He could feel his heart thumping, but was comforted by the fact that the only sounds of a dog he could hear were coming from fields beyond the yard.

Fortunately for Scab, the farm's two sheep-dogs were particularly busy that morning. One had gone with a farmworker who was feeding sheep in another part of the farm, while the second was preoccupied with what was happening in the paddock. Some of the ewes whose lambs were now sturdy enough, were being moved out to the paddock, and others that were about to lamb were being moved into the pens in the barn.

The only one to notice anything amiss was the woman who collected the duck eggs every morning. She took great pride in her seven Indian Runners, as her ducks were called, and was surprised to find that when she rooted among the straw, there wasn't an egg to be had. She also thought she got the whiff of a fox, but couldn't be sure as the smell of the dye they used to mark the lambs was strong and permeated the shed.

It was only later that the woman voiced her suspicion to her husband and, whatever about the eggs, it was agreed they couldn't risk losing any lambs. As a result, it was decided that one of their dogs would stay in the paddock, while the electric fence that divided it from the rest of the field should be switched on.

Unaware that he had aroused any suspicions, Scab made several trips down along the back of the hedge dropping the blue and pink eggs out through the fence. There they were collected by Skulking Dog and the others and taken across the river.

The duck eggs provided a rare treat, not only for the foxes, but for Whiskers and the badgers with whom they were shared, and as they licked the last traces of yolk from their noses, they were all in high spirits.

'You did well, Scab,' said Old Sage Brush. 'Very well indeed.'

Hop-along and She-la smiled, delighted that their cub was back safe and sound.

'How many dogs did you see?' asked the old fox.

'I didn't see any, I just heard one barking.'

'Did you see any cats?' asked Sinnéad.

Vickey looked at Sinnéad, then at Scab, and the two of them waited for his reply. Both vixens, the others knew, had very unpleasant memories of cats.

'No, but I got the smell of one.'

'And how many ducks did you see?' asked the old fox.

'As many as my paws, and Hop-along's.'

'What does it matter how many there were?' asked She-la, anxious to be on their way. 'We got what we wanted, didn't we?'

'We got the eggs,' said the old fox, 'but we still have to get the ducks.'

FIVE

Under the Eye of the Crow

Several grey crows had landed on fence posts near the farmhouse shortly after the first new-born lambs had been put out into the paddock.

The people on the farm watched them, knowing they could do just as much damage to their flocks as foxes, if not more. In the past few years, when foxes had been scarce, the grey crows had been their man worry, pecking the eyes out of lambs before they could stand, or out of a pregnant ewe that had gone over on her back and couldn't get up. Now they had the foxes to worry about too, but with one of the dogs in the paddock and snares in the hedges, they reckoned the lambs should be safe.

The foxes who watched from the edge of the evergreens on the other side of the river had also seen the grey crows landing on the fence posts and knew the new-born lambs that Scab had told them about were now in the paddock. They had also seen the ducks being herded into the paddock, and the black and white collie watching over them, and they realised that the task Old Sage Brush had set them wasn't going to be an easy one.

'It's so long since I've seen a duck,' said the old fox. 'Tell me Scab, are these ones white?'

Scab looked up towards the paddock again where the ducks were sifting through the mud for food. 'Just one white one. The others are brown, like the ones we sometimes find in the river. And they're not all ducks. There's a drake. He's brownish too, with a green head.'

'A green head? Or is it purple? Yes, I remember now. Drakes are like that. It's a funny colour, isn't it?"

Scab nodded. 'They've also got some other colours in their feathers, like the ones you see in the Bow in the Cloud.' Then, thinking that was a silly statement, he added, 'Sorry, I . . . I forgot, you can't see.'

'No need to apologise,' said the old fox. 'Having seen these things before, I can see them again. And you're right, some of their colours are like the ones in the bow.'

For Snout and Sniff, the flavour of egg had been the climax to a night in which they had gorged themselves on worms and beetles. Now that it was daytime, they were sleeping as they were accustomed to doing, and weren't the slightest bit concerned about how the foxes were going to get the ducks. As for Whiskers, he had gone down the river in search of eels, and was hoping that when he returned the foxes' quest for ducks would be over, and they would be ready to move on.

At the behest of the old fox, Skulking Dog and Scab had crossed the river to have another look around. Both had now returned and Skulking Dog reported that the sheep that had stuck its head through the fence had been released.

'How is that going to help us?' asked Hop–along.

'Well,' said Skulking Dog, 'in freeing the sheep, man made the hole bigger – big enough to let some of us in, I'd say.'

Hop-along grunted. 'It's not getting in you have to worry about, it's getting out.' So saying he turned and hobbled off to hunt for himself.

She-la sighed, and turning to the old fox, said, 'He's worried in case the dogs come after us. And you'd be in just as much danger as he would.'

Old Sage Brush nodded. 'I know that. But I also know we can succeed if we put our minds to it. Now, Scab, what did you see?'

'I went back up along the hedge, but only a short distance. I was going to go through it when I spotted a choking hedge-trap, so we can't get to the paddock that way.' His mother winced, and he added, 'Anyway we can approach it from the other field, now that Skulking Dog has found a way in there.'

'Tell me more about this paddock,' said the old fox. 'Where exactly is it?'

'We can see it from here,' Vickey told him. 'It's really a small field up beside the farm buildings. There's a hedge at the top and one on each side, and sheep wire along the bottom.'

'When I was up close to it,' said Scab, 'I could see straight wires running across the middle of it.'

The old fox nodded. 'I've seen man do that before. He keeps his lambs in one part until they are strong enough. Then he moves them into the other part.'

'The sheep must be very stupid,' said Scab, 'if they allow a few strands of wire to prevent them moving from one part to the other.'

'That's a special kind of wire,' Skulking Dog told him. 'If you touch it with your wet nose it gives you a dreadful jab. It's worse than the prick of a thorn.'

The fence at the bottom of the field,' said Scab, 'is one of those with small squares. Even if you could get through it, there's no way you'd get a duck back out.'

'And you'd need wings to get over it,' Stumpy remarked. 'Like those grey crows that have just landed in the tree.'

'Tree?' said the old fox. 'What tree?'

Stumpy told him that two of the grey crows had left the fence posts and were now in a beech tree that grew in a bottom corner of the field. The bottom fence was attached to it, he explained.

'What's it like?' asked the old fox.

'I told you,' said Scab. 'It's made of small squares. Like the one down near the river.'

'I don't mean the fence. The tree.'

'It's like any beech tree,' said Stumpy. 'It's got a trunk and branches, and the branches are bare, except for the crows.'

'Really now. Isn't it just as well dogs can't climb.'

Having taken their thoughts this far, the old fox curled up, and with his head on his forepaws, his nose tucked under the tip of his tail, he went to sleep.

'What did he mean?' whispered Stumpy. 'Sure we all know the dogs can't get at the crows.'

'I'm sure that's not what he meant,' said Vickey. 'But I think we should go up as far as the tree and have a look.'

'What good will that do?' asked Sinnéad. 'The ducks are with the lambs in the paddock, and the dog's keeping an eye on the lambs.'

'The ducks aren't with the lambs now,' Vickey told her. 'They've got under the wire and are feeding in the lower half of the field.'

'But what's to keep the dog from getting under the wire too?' asked She-la. 'Or jumping over it for that matter? And as Hop-along said, even if you did get the ducks how would you get them out?'

Stumpy got up to go. 'Still, Vickey's right. I think we should have a closer look.'

Skulking Dog shook his head. 'You're wasting your time. I said the hole in the fence was big enough to let some of us in. I doubt if you'd make it. I couldn't.'

'I'll go,' Scab volunteered.

'No you won't,' said She-la. 'You've done enough.'

Seeing Scab lower his head, Vickey told him, 'Your mother's right. Why don't you go with her and make sure Hop-along's all right? Perhaps I can get through the fence.' She looked at Stumpy. 'After all, there are some things a vixen can do that a bigger dog can't.'

Crossing the river, Vickey went up along the fence to the place where man had pulled at the wire to free the ewe. She found she was able to squeeze through without too much difficulty and trotted quickly up along the hedge. Arriving at a ditch she crouched behind it to take stock of the situation, and was just about to move on when she became aware of Stumpy coming up the hedge-row behind her.

'How did you get in?' she asked.

'I'm not as big as Skulking Dog. It was a tight squeeze but I managed it.'

Vickey smiled, amused at the cheek of the young fox. 'Let's hope you're not in a hurry to get back out. Anyway, I suppose two minds are better than one.'

Using the ditches for cover, they made their way up through the fields until they came to the beech tree. In the higher branches, the two grey crows saw them arrive, but didn't move; they were more interested in the lambs.

Noting that the lower branches swept down to the ground on both sides of the fence, Vickey said, 'Now do you see what Old Sage Brush meant?'

Stumpy nodded. 'I think he can see more with is inner eye than we can see with both of ours.'

'You can be sure of it,' said Vickey. 'Now. Can you see any way we might keep the dog occupied long enough to let us get the ducks?'

Peering around the tree, they could see one of the long low structures man used for feeding his sheep. There was another farther up, nearer the strands of wire that ran across the middle of the field, and they knew these structures would give them cover, if and when they went in for the ducks. Even as they watched, they heard the woman calling, 'Feedy, feedy, feedy,' and when the ducks went up into the top part of the field, they saw the black and white dog helping her herd them through the gate into the yard. A short time later, a man appeared with another dog, a brown and white one, and the sheep with lambs were taken in for the night too.

'They're taking no chances,' observed Vickey.

'No.' Stumpy shook his head. 'We're the ones that will have to do that.'

'Careful,' warned Vickey. 'The black and white dog's back.'

They watched the black and white collie run around the paddock, as if giving it one last check. Then they saw it cock its leg and widdle at the gate before disappearing into the yard.

'Do you know,' whispered Stumpy, 'I think he was laying claim to that patch of ground after the other dog was in it.'

'The question is,' said Vickey, 'How do we keep him in it long enough to get the ducks.'

'Well,' said Stumpy, 'dogs may not be like us in some ways, but they are like us in others.' And thinking of what Vickey had said earlier, he smiled and added, 'Maybe there are some things a smaller dog can do that a small vixen can't! Come on. Let's talk to Old Sage Brush.'

Darkness enveloped the valley, and the moon came up. The badgers scurried around in search of their food, and the foxes discussed how they were going to get theirs.

As Vickey and Stumpy related what they had seen and what they proposed to do, the others listened with great interest, nodding when they agreed with some point, looking up at the night sky when they were in doubt. Whatever about Vickey's part of the plan, some of them had grave reservations about what Stumpy was proposing. However, Old Sage Brush had also been listening and he liked what he had heard.

The plan provided that the raid should be carried out by Stumpy and the three vixens, and after the vixens had talked it over among themselves, She-la announced, 'All right, we'll give it a try. But only if the rest of you go on ahead and wait for us.'

'I know a place where they can hide farther down the river,' said Whiskers. 'I've travelled the path, and there are no hedge-traps to worry about.' He dashed off, then stopped to tell them, 'I'll get the badgers and let them know what we're doing.'

'Well,' said Skulking Dog, 'since I can't get through the fence, I'll go with Old Sage Brush and make sure he's all right.'

Sinnéad smiled in a way that said thanks, and She-la added, 'Fine. Scab will go with Hop-along, and they all should have plenty of time to get there before we make our move.'

Just before dawn, Stumpy followed the three vixens across the river and, in accordance with their plan, She-la waited on the bank outside the fence. Stumpy was the last to go in, and as she shoved him through she wondered, just as Vickey had wondered, what he would do if he was in a hurry to get back out.

Stumpy caught up with the other two vixens at the base of the beech tree. There were already some early morning sounds coming from the direction of the farm buildings, but still no sign of the lambs, or the ducks.

'Better go while the going's good,' said Vickey.

Stumpy hopped on to a long low branch that swept down from the tree and climbed up along it. At one point he seemed to lose his balance for a moment, and the vixens wondered if it was because he had no tail. Then they saw him making his way down a branch on the other side, and hopping into the field.

'Good luck,' whispered Sinnéad.

Vickey took a deep breath and added, 'He'll need it.'

From the side of the first sheep feeder, Stumpy could see that the top half of the field was still empty. Keeping low, he sped up to the next one and took cover behind it. The sounds from the farm were getting louder, and he reckoned it was now or never. Dashing up to the fence with the straight strands of wire, he stopped at one of the posts. Like cows and other animals, he could smell the electricity the wires carried. Taking great care not to touch the lower one, he cocked his leg and widdled around the bottom of the post. In his excitement he thought it was just as well he didn't have a tail, otherwise he might have touched the wire with that. Returning to the cover of the feeder, he waited to see what would happen. Once he had seen a dog widdle where a cat had been, but it was only when he had seen this dog make its mark that he realised how much they indulged in this habit. Maybe, he thought, it would react to a fox's mark in the same way.

Down at the beech tree, the vixens watched with much amusement. They were also hoping that the plan would work.

After a short time the ewes with lambs were brought back into the paddock, and as the black and white sheep-dog lay and watched them, Stumpy hoped against hope it wouldn't find his mark before the ducks arrived. Fortunately, the wind was blowing down towards him, and knowing the dog was unlikely to get his scent, he sat tight. Behind him he became aware of the grey crows returning to the beech tree, but knew they wouldn't draw attention to their presence in the way rooks would.

It wasn't' long before a loud quacking told the foxes that the ducks were on their way too. For what seemed a long time, they moved around the top half of the field, waddling here and there as they sought out worms and other food with their flat bills. Then the empty part of the field seemed to beckon them, and gradually they made their way down under the strands of wire.

Seeing them go, the dog followed as far as the fence and immediately picked up the scent of the fox. Excited, it ran along the wire until it came to the post where Stumpy had left his mark. There it proceeded to superimpose its mark but it wasn't as careful as Stumpy had been. In spraying the bottom of the post, it also hit the lower strand of wire, and an electric shock sent it jumping backward with yelp.

Pickling itself up, it ran back up the field, howling with pain as it went, and hopped over the gate into the yard. Seeing that the way was clear, the vixens made their way across the branches of the beech tree as quickly as balance would allow, streaked towards the ducks at a dizzy speed and without stopping, scooped up one each.

Stumpy waited until they had negotiated their way back up the branch, and when he saw them safely on the other side, he also headed for the ducks. However, as he swerved around them, he became aware of the brown and white dog streaking down the field behind him. Annoyed with himself that he had forgotten about the second dog, he scooped up the drake and headed for the beech tree. Out of the corner of his eye he could see the dog jumping the electric fence and racing after him at full stretch. The duck was awkward to carry and slowing him down. For a moment he wondered if he should drop it. Then he found himself at the tree and jumped up on to the branch. He could hear the dogs' teeth snapping behind him, and thanked his lucky stars that he didn't have a tail. The branch was swaying, and the dog was jumping up at him. He kept going, and somehow managed to maintain his balance long enough to reach a firmer footing where the branch met the trunk. There he turned and looked down at the dog. It was sitting back, its teeth bared, looking up at him, and even though it continued to jump, he knew and it knew it was jumping in vain.

Hearing a shout from the farmyard gate, Stumpy hopped into the field on the other side of the tree and ran down along the hedge. Someone, he knew was shouting at the dog, and had he known what it was being told, he might even have felt sorry for it. Thinking that the dog was barking at the crows, man was telling it to leave them be, that it was wasting its time!

Down at the river, She-la helped Stumpy get the duck through the fence, and when he had squeezed through himself, they raced away after Vickey and Sinnéad. Farther down the river, Whiskers picked them up and led them to where the others were hiding.

'Two ducks and a drake,' said the old fox. 'Not bad. And what about man? Did he give chase?'

Stumpy laughed. 'He didn't, but one of his dogs did. I think it was disappointed when it couldn't catch me by the tail.'

Vickey smiled. 'It's just as well dogs can't climb, or we'd all be in trouble.'

'So man may not even know he's lost any ducks?' said Hop-along.

'Not yet,' said Sinnéad. 'But he'll know when he takes them in for the night.'

Old Sage Brush, who was enjoying his long-awaited taste of duck, chuckled. 'And I suppose, Scab, if he ever does come looking for them, all he will find is the colours of the bow?'

Scab looked at the mounting pile of feathers and replied, 'That's about all.'

SIX

Spirits of the Night

A light mist wreathed the meadows in white, and the only sound to break the stillness of the night was the occasional gurgle of the river as it made its way to what Whiskers called the Edge of the World.

'It's funny how you get used to the sound of the river,' said Vickey.

They had made themselves a den in a clump of withered ferns beneath a copse of alder and birch trees. Behind them, the fields sloped up, more gently now, and in front of them was the bank which had become ragged and deeper as the river wended its way through the valley.

'The river talks to us,' replied Old Sage Brush. 'It's a living thing and like all living things it tells us much about itself.' He thought about it for a moment, and continued, 'Earlier on, when it was young, it was frisky, for I could hear it giggle and play like a cub that had just emerged from its earth, full of the joys of life. Later, as it got a little older, I could tell from its sounds that it was getting stronger, still not sure of itself, but preparing to make its mark. Then it became quieter, and I knew it was becoming bigger and more mature, carving out a territory for itself as it moved farther from its home.'

'We are far from home now too,' said Sinnéad. 'We must also travel quietly and with greater care.' She was relieved that their raid on the sheep farm, with all the dangers it held, was now well behind them, and was hoping that the old fox had got over the mood that had led them to undertake it.

Sensing that this was what she meant, Old Sage Brush remarked, 'Care must govern all our actions.'

Before he could say anything more, the silence of the meadows was broken by a shriek, a shriek that man would consider to be even more frightening than the cry of a vixen. The older foxes, however, knew it to be the signal that others were about to embark on a night's hunting, and a short time later they saw the white figures of two barn owls gliding silently across the misty meadows.

Scab, who hadn't seen barn owls before, thought they were very weird. They reminded him of some of the stories he had heard from his parents as a very young cub, and he remarked, 'They're like the spirits of the night.'

'I cannot see them,' said Old Sage Brush, 'But when I could they reminded me of the spirits of the afterlife, flying over that other world we know as the happy hunting ground.'

Sinnéad didn't like to hear her father talking like that so she said, 'Why speak of death when we are alive? Haven't we hunted the Sheep Lands as you wished? Sipped the eggs and savoured the duck? What more could you wish for?'

'It is true,' replied the old fox, 'we have taken the eggs from under the eye of man, and the ducks from under the eye of the grey crow. But the grey crow still lives.'

Seeing the look of despair in Sinnéad's eyes, Vickey said, 'Why should we worry about the grey crow? Man will attend to it as he always does, and on our return we will find it hanging out to dry.'

'I know man will kill the grey crow,' the old fox told her, 'but it is we who must avenge the deaths of our brothers and sisters who lie on the bog. Those same brothers and sisters whose spirits now glide over the other world, searching for the things they can never have in this one. They have lost their eyes to the grey crow, while the grey crow still casts its greedy eyes on the lambs.

The two badgers, who had been grubbing for food along the river bank, came lumbering back, and as they settled down beside the old fox, the vixens moved out of earshot to talk among themselves.

'He won't be happy until we get the grey crows too,' declared Sinnéad. 'I've never seen him in such a stubborn mood. Never.'

Vickey smiled. 'You mustn't be too hard on him. He feels very strongly about what happened to those foxes on the bog.'

They stopped talking and looked up as the two barn owls glided silently over their heads and disappeared into the mist.

'I think it's the injustice of it all that's getting to him,' said She-la. 'I mean, they can't all have been killing lambs. I'm sure the crows did their share of the damage, and yet they lived to feed upon the foxes too.'

Vickey nodded. 'Then the sooner we figure out a way of getting them, the better.'

Having eaten his fill of worms and beetles, the boar badger was now lying on his back beside Old Sage Brush, scratching his belly, while his mate was nibbling at the fur on her hind leg as she carefully groomed herself.

'Well Snout,' said the old fox, 'I hope those are not fleas that are making you scratch.'

The boar smiled, and rolling back on to his paws, said, 'No, no fleas. When you've eaten well, it just feels good to lie back and have a good scratch. Isn't that right Sniff?' His mate smiled, and he went on, 'But speaking of fleas, your friend back at Beech Paw seems to have his fair share of them.'

Old Sage Brush laughed. 'You mean Ratwiddle? I suppose he has all right.'

The sow badger sniffed and said, 'He has some strange thoughts in his mind as well.'

Old Sage Brush nodded.

'I wonder what he meant?' asked Snout. 'I mean, how can man walk upon the water? How can the caterpillar hunt man? And how can rats hunt the fox? I have never heard of such a thing.'

'I just hope it doesn't mean more trouble for us,' said Sniff. 'We've had all the trouble we can take.'

'There is usually some explanation for the things that Ratwiddle sees in his tortured mind,' the old fox told them, 'but don't concern yourselves too much about it.

If something is hunting man it will be a change from man hunting us, and if rats hunt the fox, then that will be our problem.'

Sniff came closer and, looking at the ld fox as if she was intent on studying his reaction, recalled, 'Your friend the otter said something equally strange. He said that at the Edge of the World, man has been known to feed the badger. How can that be when all he has ever done to us is kill and maim?'

'Man is not easy to understand,' replied Old Sage Brush. 'The young fox we told you about, the one back in the Land of Sinna, he was the pet of man and the friend of dogs.'

Hearing this, Vickey came over to them, and settling down beside the old fox, recalled, 'Needle Nine had very sharp teeth and was always chewing things, but man cared for him just the way he cares for his dogs.'

'But have you ever known man to care for a badger?' asked Sniff.

Old Sage Brush shook his head. 'I have lived for many seasons and I have seen many things, but now that you ask me, I must say I have never known man to care for a badger. I have seen him dig the badger out of its sett, and I've seen him cage it. I've seen him set his dogs upon it and I've seen him kill it. But feed it? No. And yet, the otter has travelled farther than I have. He has seen many things that even I have not seen, and I have no reason to doubt what he says.'

'But man feeding badgers?' said Snout. 'It's just so hard to imagine, after all the horrible things we've seen him do.'

The other foxes had gathered round now, and Hop-along asked, 'Why does man hunt you the way he does? Is it for your fur, or . . . ?'

'For food?' Snout laughed and shook his head. 'No. But according to the stories that were handed down from one generation to another in our sett, there was a time when he did hunt us for food. Not any more. He doesn't even seem to be interested in our fur.'

'And a fine coat of fur it is too,' said Vickey.

'Although . . . there is a story told in badgerlore,' recalled Sniff. 'I . . . remember hearing it from my grand-mother when I was a cub. She said man did have a use for our fur once, but I didn't really understand it. She said he used it to get rid of his own fur.'

'I never knew man had fur,' said Scab.

'Sometimes he has fur on his head,' his mother told him.'

'And sometimes he hasn't.' Hop-along smiled. 'From what I've seen of man, it can be a bit patchy, like your own!'

Scab laughed and seeing that he wasn't offended by his father's remark, the others laughed too.

'I once saw man with fur on his chin,' said Stumpy. 'He was on a horse following the howling dogs.'

'Fur on his chin?' Old Sage Brush chuckled. 'Wait until Whiskers hears about that.'

'Well, it wasn't really like the whiskers Whiskers has,' said Stumpy. 'It was fuzzy, like fur.'

They had another good laugh at that, and then Scab asked, 'But if you were being chased by the howling dogs, how did you get so close to man to see the fur on his chin?'

'It was the last thing I saw,' said Stumpy, '. . . before he cut off my tail.'

Their laughter seemed oddly out of place now, and as they lapsed into silence, Old Sage Brush turned to the boar badger and said, 'Tell me about your sett, Snout. You said it went back many generations?'

Knowing that once her mate got started, he and the old fox were likely to talk long into the night, Sniff shuffled off to forage for more food. The other foxes listened for a while, but soon it became obvious that this was talk for older, wiser heads, so they too slipped away and left them to it. Anyway, they had things of their own to talk about. They were all conscious of the need to get away from the Land of the Sheep and the dangers it held for them. They also knew that until they figured out a way to get the grey crow, Old Sage Brush would be dragging his feet and making things difficult for them.

'His obstinacy knows no bounds,' said Sinnéad, 'even when he is in danger.'

Vickey smiled. 'He has great faith in his own kind and in the cunning the great god Vulpes has given us. That's why he feels so badly about what happened to our brothers and sisters on the bog.'

They discussed the situation at length and were still pondering the problem of the grey crows, when the sow badger returned. As she lay down beside them, she raised her nose and sniffed, and they wondered if this was just a habit, or if she was sniffing the scents of the night.

'Back at Beech Paw,' she ventured shyly, 'you spoke of the Bow in the Cloud. You said that when ever it appeared it was a sign that the creatures of the earth would somehow survive.' The others nodded, and she asked, 'Does that include badgers?'

'It includes all creatures,' She-la assured her.

'I have heard Old Sage Brush speak of it often,' said Sinnéad, 'even though he cannot see it.'

Sniff lowered her head and smiled at her. 'You're his daughter, aren't you?'

Sinnéad nodded. 'I was the only member of the litter to survive when man and his dogs dug us from our earth. They found out where we were by pushing long sticks down through the sand. He refused to give our position away even though the sticks were blinding him. But I couldn't let them do that to him. I caught one of the sticks . . . and then they knew where we were. But . . . ' She shook her head, 'that's another story.'

Seeing that these were very painful memories for Sinnéad, Sniff said, 'But the story of the Bow in the Cloud. Tell me about that.'

'When we were young,' Sinnéad recalled, 'he used to show it to us, and tell us how it came to be there.'

There was silence beneath the mist, the silence of hunting owls that produced uneasy shuffling in the hedge-rows, the silence of a river that gurgled its way to the Edge of the World – the true silence of natural sounds that told the foxes man was not around. Content in the knowledge that they were safe, for the moment at any rate, the younger foxes edged closer to hear Sinnéad tell a story they had heard many times before.

'Long ago,' she said, 'a great disaster befell the world, a disaster greater than anything we have ever known.'

'Greater than the fire in the fields?' asked Scab.

Sinnéad nodded.

'Greater than the flood that came to the Land of Sinna?' asked Stumpy.

Sinnéad nodded again. 'Much greater. And many creatures died.

'More than died on the bog? asked Sniff.

'Many more. More than have died in the jaws of the howling dogs; more than have ever died at the hands of man.'

Hop-along shifted uneasily as he thought of how he would have died in the jaws of man's trap, had he not chewed off his own paw to escape.

'The beasts of the fields and the birds of the air, they all died,' Sinnéad continued.

'All of them?' asked Stumpy.

'Only two of each were left,' said Sinnéad. 'Only two of each in the whole world, and they were given a sign.'

'The Bow in the Cloud,' said Scab.

Sinnéad nodded. 'When it appeared, they were told, it would be a sign that whatever great disaster had befallen them, the like of it would never happen again.'

'But perhaps the bow is only meant for those who hunt by day and can see it,' said Sniff. 'We are creatures of the night.'

Vickey smiled and assured her, 'We are told that it is a sign for all creatures, whether they swim like the otter, fly like the owl, crawl like the beetle, grub like the badger or hunt like the fox.'

Skulking dog, who liked nothing better than raiding a hen house, said, 'I often wonder if it's a sign that we'll always have chickens. It seems to me they're getting very scarce.'

'And I wonder if it means we'll always have rabbits?' wondered Hop-along. 'It would be a pity if they died out.'

She-la nodded to show she agreed with her mate, and said, 'I wonder if man sees it as a sign?'

'If he does,' said Sniff, 'he doesn't seem to pay much heed to it. Look what he did to your brothers and sisters on the bog. Look what he did to us. Our family, our sett, our whole way of life – all gone in one night. but then perhaps he does these awful things when others can't see him and the bow isn't there to remind him that we should be left alone.'

The sow badger lowered her head to hide her tears, and they knew they would have to wait until another time to hear about the dreadful disaster that had befallen her sett back in the Land of the Cow.

The hunting owls glided silently over their heads once more like the spirits of the night, reminding the foxes of the tragedy that had befallen their own kind, and the old fox's wish that they do something about the grey crow. The owls also reminded them that they too should have been out hunting, but while man slept, his choking hedge-traps guarded his sheep, and they knew they would have to wait until morning before venturing out in search of food.

One by one they dozed off, taking memories from the past and fears for the future into their dreams – and whatever shape those thoughts took in the private world of sleep, it seemed to end almost before it had started. Suddenly Whiskers came crashing in upon them, and they awoke with a start to find him looking down on them from an early dawn.

'You gave us an awful fright,' said Vickey.

'Just as well I wasn't' a sheep-dog,' replied the otter. They could see he was dripping wet and out of breath.

'Sheep-dogs don't come out of the river,' said Sinnéad.

Ignoring her rebuke, Whiskers shook himself vigorously. Instinctively, they stepped back from the droplets of water that were showered upon them, but before they could protest, he panted, 'There's a fox up in the sheep fields, I think it's gone crazy.'

'Where?' asked Skulking Dog.'

Looking around them, they saw that the mist had lifted.

'In the slopes behind you. Look, over there.'

They could see the fox now, zig-zagging among the sheep.

'It must have been eating the wrong mushrooms,' remarked Hop-along.

'Toadstools, more likely,' added She-la.

Some of the sheep were heavy with lamb, but hadn't been taken into the more securely-wired areas where lambing would take place.

'If the farmer sees it, it'll be shot,' said Vickey.

Skulking Dog nodded. 'If the dogs don't find it first.'

'And if it runs this way, we'll all be in trouble,' warned She-la.

Old Sage Brush and Snout were still asleep a short distance away, unaware of what was happening, and as Sinnéad and Sniff went to alert them, Skulking Dog said, 'Come on Stumpy. We'll see if we can head this crazy fox off. The rest of you, make your way on down the river until you find a safe place. We'll catch up with you.'

The others hesitated.

'Hurry!' urged Skulking Dog.

Vickey nodded to the others. 'Go on, I'll follow you.'

She-la, Hop-along and Scab took off, and turning to the two other dog foxes, Vickey told them, 'Be careful. And watch out for choking hedge-traps.'

She watched Skulking Dog and Stumpy cross the first ditch and as they disappeared over it with the flick of only one brush, she couldn't help thinking, even in this moment of crisis how odd Stumpy looked without a tail. Then she hurried off to make sure Old Sage Brush and the others were on their way to safety.

Hoping against hope that the bleating of the frightened sheep wouldn't bring the dogs down upon them, Skulking Dog and Stumpy took a chance and ran straight across the open fields until they came to where the crazy fox was trying desperately to get in through a sheep fence.

'What are you doing?' asked Skulking Dog.

Almost as if it didn't hear him, the strange fox turned, took a rather uncertain course down the field, and attacked the fence again. It was, they could see, in a dreadful condition. Its coat had lost all lustre and in places had fallen away to reveal the smallness of a body that had somehow been reduced to skin and bone. Its eyes bulged from its head as if it was crazed with hunger, and its brush, which was wet and skinny, trailed along the ground as if it hadn't the strength to carry it.

'You'll get us all killed,' said Stumpy.

There were other places where a fox in such an emaciated condition could have got through the fence, but it continued to try to push its muzzle into places where it was plain to see it couldn't possibly get through.

'Come with us,' urged Skulking Dog. 'Maybe we can help you.'

The strange fox didn't respond, and they realised it was too far gone to hear, think, or even be aware that they were trying to help it.

'Let's see if we can steer it away from here,' said Skulking Dog.

Stumpy glanced back over his shoulder and was relieved to see that the only eyes watching them were those of the sheep. They had crowded together in nervous little knots a short distance away and were uttering an occasional frightened bleat in a mixture of curiosity and fear.

Skulking Dog rushed at the strange fox and bowled it over. However, it didn't react as they thought a crazy fox might. Instead of attacking them, it picked itself up

73

and trotted off across the field, taking an erratic course that clearly showed it didn't know what it was doing or where it was going.

Now, for the first time, Skulking Dog and Stumpy could see that the wire of a choking hedge-trap protruded from a festering circle on its neck, sticking up in the air in such a grotesque way that it reminded them of a lead on a dog held by an invisible hand.

Recovering from their shock, they were on either side of the fox in an instant, and in this way guided it down to the river. There, under cover of the ferns, they talked to it again, not expecting a response this time, but telling it they were taking it to safety and hoping it would understand.

Whiskers and the badgers were no less horrified than the other foxes when the thin, pathetic figure that had been choked to the point of death by man's inhumanity was helped into the undergrowth where they had taken cover. How, they wondered, could he do such a dreadful thing to one of his fellow creatures? How could he allow any living thing to be reduced to such a pitiable state?

'It's like a walking skeleton,' Vickey told Old Sage Brush. 'You would hardly know it was a fox. And yet, I've a feeling I've seen it somewhere before . . . '

SEVEN

A Race Against Time

Perhaps it was a good omen. The colours of the bow had been seen on the river. Just a flash, Scab reported, but where else could such brilliance have come from, except the Bow in the Cloud? Yet there was no cloud. The sky was clear. Nor was there any sun. It was cold, and the ice of winter was not far off.

'What colour was it, exactly?' Old Sage Brush asked him.

'It's difficult to say.'

'Did it have the green of the drake?'

'That's it, it was green.' Scab thought for a moment. 'Or was it blue?'

'Make up your mind,' said Stumpy. 'It can't have been both.'

'The Bow in the Cloud is all colours,' the old fox reminded him.

Stumpy looked at the sky. 'I can't see anything.'

'I was looking at the river,' said Scab. 'And look, there it is again.'

By the time Stumpy looked, there was nothing to be seen, but Whiskers who always watched the river, smiled, saying, 'Only one thing can bring the colours of the bow to the river, and that's the kingfisher. There it is, over there.'

Whiskers pointed with his snout to an alder tree that clung rather tenuously to the river bank, and there the young foxes saw a dumpy little bird with a long beak and short tail. Blue, green, brown, red — it seemed its feathers had all the colours of the bow. Even its legs were bright red. Next moment it was gone, and the flash of colour Scab had reported appeared on the river as it hit the water and returned to its perch with a stickleback in its beak.

The kingfisher banged the small fish against the branch, and when Scab remarked on the way it swallowed it head first, Old Sage Brush said to him, 'Remember the time I took you to the river? When you were just a cub? I told you that you must swallow fish head first like the kingfisher, otherwise the bones will get stuck in your throat.'

'That's right!' exclaimed Scab. 'And you showed us how to walk in the water, like the dipper.'

'There are other things you can learn from these two birds,' the old fox added. 'You too Stumpy.'

There was another flash of colour on the river as the kingfisher dived again.

'The kingfisher is not unlike us,' Old Sage Brush continued. 'It digs a tunnel in the river bank, just the way we dig an earth, and there it makes its nest. But the brilliance of its flight is not matched by the brilliance of its mind.'

'How come?' asked Stumpy.

'Because it leaves the remains of its fish and the waste of its young around the opening of the tunnel for all to see. A bit like us, wouldn't' you say?'

The young foxes nodded, and Scab said, 'But you allowed us to leave the feathers of the ducks where man could see them'

'That's because I wanted him to see them,' the old fox replied. 'I wanted him to know it was his ducks we were after, not his lambs. Anyway, we were on the move. Leaving them around an earth is a different matter, and you might do well to remember it.'

'That is a mistake the dipper will not make,' Whiskers told them. 'You may see it walking on the water, but it will take great pains to remove all traces of waste from the entrance to its nest.'

'But you leave your mark for others to see, just as we do,' Scab told Whiskers.

'And you leave the remains of your food on the river bank for all to see,' added Stumpy.

'True,' said Whiskers, 'but when it comes to my den there is noting to see. The opening is under the water.'

The old fox smiled, and getting up, said, 'Let's see if the vixens are having any success with our unfortunate friend. I'd say he hasn't left much trace of food for a long time.'

In a patch of scrub not too far from the river bank, they found the vixens still wondering what to do with the injured fox.

'What do you think?' asked Old Sage Brush.

'He's lying down now,' Vickey informed him. She lowered her voice. 'But I just don't know how we're going to get the wire off his neck.'

'So it's a dog fox? What age is he?'

'I don't know. He's in such a dreadful condition, it's impossible to say.'

The injured fox was lying on his side, his head on the ground, his eyes bulging. His tongue was hanging out, and the rapid rise and fall of his ribs underlined his distress.

She-la was lying beside him, talking quietly to him, and Sinnéad said to the old fox. 'I don't know if he can understand what we're saying, but he can hear us and it's having a calming effect on him.'

'Once, Vickey,' said the old fox, 'when your mate, Black Tip got caught in a choking hedge-trap, our friend with the long teeth, what was his name?'

'Fang.'

'That's right, Fang was able to get his teeth under the wire and loosen it out.'

Vickey shook her head. 'There's not a hope. Not this time. The wire's embedded so deeply in his neck he can barely breathe.'

'That means he can't eat,' said the old fox. 'Little wonder he was acting the way he was. The hunger must have been driving him crazy.'

Skulking Dog was looking at the ragged end of the wire. 'He must have put up a great fight to break it.'

'It's a wonder it didn't choke him,' said Stumpy.

Vickey nodded. 'It practically has. He has suffered an awful lot.'

'We too suffer from the choking hedge-traps,' said Snout, 'but, maybe it's because of the way we're made, they usually end up around our bodies.'

'Because we are strong,' explained Sniff, 'we struggle very hard and they cause great injuries inside our bodies.'

'Injuries,' added Snout, 'that man cannot see.'

Hop-along, who had been studying the wire protruding from the neck of the other fox, wondered if in fact it had been intended for a badger. 'Look how strong it is,' he observed. 'It stands up on its own.'

'And yet he managed to break it,' said Skulking Dog.

Whatever about the younger foxes, the others, and indeed the badgers, knew from bitter experience that man usually made his snares in such a way that no matter how much an animal might twist and turn, it wouldn't break. The reason for this, a reason beyond the comprehension of the animals it frustrated, was that the wire turned on a swivel. In this instance, however, the trapper had omitted the swivel in the mistaken belief that the wire was strong enough to hold any animal, be it badger or fox.

Sniff shuffled forward to have a closer look. 'It is strong, isn't it?' She eyed it up and down. 'You don't think we could push it back through the loop, do you?'

'Now there's an idea,' said Old Sage Brush. 'What do you think, Vickey?'

'It's difficult to say. It's so deeply embedded in his neck.'

'Sinnéad?'

Sinnéad shook her head. 'I don't know if he could stand the pain.'

'She-la?'

'She-la's still talking to him,' said Hop-along. 'But if we don't do something he's going to die.'

'Perhaps if we could get him down to the river,' suggested Whiskers, 'we could wash the wound and give it a try.'

'I think he has gone as far as he can go,' said Vickey.

Sinnéad nodded. 'So do I.'

Vickey went over, and getting down beside She-la, told the stricken fox, 'We're going to try to get the wire off your neck.' There was no reply, and she continued, 'It's going to hurt, but there's no other way.' There was still no response, and turning to the others, she said, 'Well, who's going to do it?'

'Perhaps, Skulking Dog,' said the old fox, 'if the vixens hold him down, you might try it.'

She-la rested her muzzle gently on the fox's ear and whispered comforting words into it, while Vickey and Sinnéad rested their heads, equally gently, on his heaving body.

Skulking Dog hesitated for a moment, then made his way quietly around to where the wire of the snare rested on the ground. Opening his mouth, he pushed his lower jaw under it.

The injured fox twitched. Slowly he closed his teeth on the wire, and pushed it firmly towards the neck. With a heart-rending cry of pain, pain that those around him could almost feel themselves, the injured fox struggled to his feet.

For a moment they thought he was going to take off but almost immediately he collapsed in a heap and there wasn't' another sound or movement from him.

'Is he dead?' asked Stumpy.

'If he's not, he's not far from it,' said She-la.

'Dead or alive,' the old fox told them, 'he won't feel anything now. Keep going.'

Skulking Dog continued to push the wire towards the neck of the motionless fox, but his teeth kept slipping up along it.

'Here, maybe I can get a grip on it,' said Snout.

Relieved that someone else was going to try, and knowing that no other animal had stronger jaws than a badger, Skulking Dog stepped aside.

'Hold him steady now,' Snout told the vixens, and grasping the wire firmly between his teeth, close to where it circled the neck, he pushed and pushed until She-la exclaimed. 'It's moving! Keep going, it's moving!'

Snout adjusted his grip and pushed and pushed until, almost like a miracle, the wire began to rise up out of the festering circle. She-la immediately caught it and pulled it out through the tiny loop that had held it so tightly. Snout then nudged the unconscious head up so that she could get her nose underneath, and after a little more pushing and pulling, she managed to drag the wire clear.

'Is he going to live?' Scab asked She-la.

His mother looked at him and smiled. 'Who can say? We've done all we can.' Picking up the wire, she trotted off to a nearby clearing where, with the help of Sniff, she dug a deep trench and buried it. Both badger and fox were united in their determination that this contraption of man should never again cause suffering to any living creature.

The evening was getting cold, and sensing that a frost was going to set in, Old Sage Brush said, 'All we can do now is to keep him warm . . . and hope.'

Now, for the first time, they realised that they had been so preoccupied with the stricken fox, they had forgotten to hunt. However, when they felt the bones of the frail body that lay between them, they knew it was more important to look after one who had not eaten for a long time.

Almost before it was dark, the moon came up, a large round moon that seemed to smile on what they had done, and it bathed the limp body that lay in their midst in the comforting half-light of gloomglow. Perhaps they may have looked upon it as a healing glow, the glow of a great caring eye that was the same colour as their own. Perhaps fate, in the person of the moon, was smiling upon them. Who knows? Whatever it was, an unspoken feeling now spread among them that life might flow back into the strangled body that had been placed in their care.

These thoughts, of course, may seem strange to man. But man doesn't know everything. He knows that foxes have a great capacity to recover from injury. Even when they break a leg he knows they can survive without food until the broken parts fuse together. However, he doesn't know everything, and when those beneath the scrub went to sleep that night, they were hungry but not without hope.

Next morning, the moon lingered in the sky, almost as though it was waiting to see if the glow with which it had cloaked the stricken fox had helped him through the night. Even as it waited, a sudden intake of breath stirred the other foxes, and they awoke to find their injured companion gulping for air. Then, before they realised what was happening, he jumped to his feet and ran off through the scrub.

It was a moment or two before they got over their surprise, and when they did, She-la and Sinnéad, who had been lying beside him, jumped up and ran after him. Their first thought was that he might head for the sheep fields again, but when they caught up with him, he was standing in a patch of gravel at the edge of the river, lapping up the water.

Vickey was close behind, followed by others, and as she explained to Old Sage Brush what was happening, She-la was saying, 'Are you all right? Are you feeling any better?'

The injured fox made no reply, but staggered back out to the bank and sank to the ground beside them.

Vickey smiled. 'He *is* feeling better. He *is*. All he needs now is time.'

They helped him back to their den in the scrub, and as they discussed who would hunt where, Old Sage Brush said, 'It will probably be a while yet before he can eat. But if he can wait, so can we.'

Sinnéad approached the old fox, saying, 'But we must be on our way. Those sheep Skulking Dog and Stumpy saw were close to their lambing time.'

'She's right,' said Vickey. 'The grey crows are already gathering. I saw one this morning.'

'But you yourself said all our friend here needs is time,' replied the old fox, 'and perhaps the time we need to catch the grey crow will be time enough for him.'

Knowing that they were wasting their time arguing, the vixens returned to the injured fox, while Skulking Dog and Stumpy went off to forage for food. The others would take their turn later, but for the moment it was enough that two foxes should be hunting in sheep country.

As the badgers had mentioned at the outset, it wasn't in their nature to travel far, let alone in daylight, and now that Old sage Brush had called a halt, they reverted to their old habit of sleeping during the day and eating at night.

'Snout,' said the old fox when he heard the sow badger making a den in the undergrowth, 'we are in your debt for what you have done.'

Snout raised his nose in the air and replied, 'What have I done but help you, just as you are helping us?'

'You and your mate have saved a life, the life of one who is not of your kind. And that is a noble thing to do.'

Snout dismissed his thanks with a snort, and when he shuffled off to join his mate, Old Sage Brush settled down to listen to what the vixens were saying to the injured fox.

'How is he?' he asked after a while.

'He's better now that the wire has gone from his neck,' replied She-la. 'But it's a race against time. He needs to eat to live, and he can't eat until he can swallow.'

'Whiskers thinks the water will help to heal his wound,' said the old fox. 'Next time he goes to the river, why don't you help him wash the pain away.'

So it was that the vixens soothed the circle of pain on the neck of their stricken friend, and by talking to him, soothed his tortured mind, and in the days and nights that followed, the healing process worked faster than his starvation. Gradually he began to eat. Starting with soft slugs, which he found he could swallow without too much pain, he soon moved on to other things, and it became a matter of great joy for the others to see him try bits and pieces they had brought back from their hunting trips.

Gradually too, the injured fox began to improve in appearance. It would be a while before his coat started to grow again, but his brush was taking on a fulsomeness that showed he was gaining in strength. At the same time, his eyes ceased to bulge, his ears became erect, and to their surprise, his face took on the slender look of a young fox.

For all that, he couldn't talk, and so they talked to him.

They told him of life in the Land of Sinna, of the journey they were making to the Edge of the World with Whiskers, how they had got the eggs from the sheep farm, and how they had figured out a way to get the ducks that had the colours of the bow. They also told him that some day soon they planned to catch the grey crow.

Then, one evening as they discussed these plans, he cleared his throat, and croaking like a crow himself, said, 'But I didn't think hunting would be so difficult.'

'You can talk?' exclaimed Vickey. 'You can talk!'

'Of course he can talk,' said Old Sage Brush. 'It was just a matter of time.'

'When we were talking to you about the Land of Sinna,' Vickey continued, 'you knew about it, didn't you? I could tell by your reaction.'

The other fox nodded.

'That's because you're from there, isn't it?'

'That's right.' He coughed to clear his throat. 'I'm Needle Nine.'

EIGHT

An Eye for an Eye

The cold of evening gripped the countryside in a hand of ice, and as Vickey cast her thoughts back home to the Land of Sinna, she couldn't help thinking how cruel fate had been to the young cub she had known as Needle Nine. Perhaps it was because she remembered him as such a fine young cub, a cub full of the joys of life and, unusually for a fox, full of confidence in man. It was her mate, Black Tip, and Skulking Dog who had first spotted him, living on a farm with man and his dogs. Later, he had slipped away and come up to Beech Paw to see her. There, when she was expecting cubs of her own, she had told him about things his mother would have told him, such as the Great Running Fox in the Sky and how it had guided them on another journey before he was born. When the injured fox told her who he was, therefore, she could scarcely believe it.

'But what happened to you?' she asked when she got over the shock. 'You were man's pet. How did you come to be in this mess?'

'Leave him be,' said the old fox. 'It's probably a long story. He can tell us another time, when he's stronger.'

Needle Nine coughed again, and croaked, 'It was very simple really.' The others crowded closer to hear.

'Man was very good to me, but as I got bigger I suppose I became a bit of a nuisance. And one day . . . ' He coughed again. 'One day they decided to give me my freedom. However, they didn't know that I couldn't hunt. My parents had been killed, you see. That's why they took me in, in the first place... and I never learned how to hunt. It's as simple as that.' He coughed gently again to clear his throat. 'I didn't know the ways of the wild, and one day I ended up in the choking hedge-trap. I don't know how long I was in it, but I twisted and twisted until it broke.' He coughed again. 'By that time it had closed so tightly on my throat I could hardly breathe.'

'But how did you manage to eat?' asked Hop-along.

'I didn't.' He coughed. 'I couldn't. I could only drink. That kept me going for a while. But soon I became desperate. The hunger. The pain. I couldn't bear it. It drove me out of my mind. I didn't know what I was doing.'

'When we found you up in the sheep fields,' said Skulking Dog, 'you were trying to get in through the fence.'

'The sheep fields? I wonder what I was doing up there?'

'Who knows?' said Sinnéad gently. 'But don't worry. It's all over now.'

'But I still can't hunt,' admitted Needle Nine. 'And it all sounds so complicated.'

'If you care to come with us,' said Old Sage Brush, 'we will show you how to hunt. And it need not be complicated. Take, for instance, the grey crow. The time has come to catch it. Now Scab, what was that you were saying about a fox in sheep's clothing?'

Scab laughed. 'It was just something that occurred to me when I was in the shed watching the ducks. Man had taken the fur of the sheep and hung it up on the wall. I was just thinking that if we could get one of those and hide under it, like a sheep, we might be able to take the grey crow unawares.'

'That's ridiculous,' said She-la. 'Even if we could reach it, we'd never get it out without the dogs seeing us.'

'Your mother's right,' said the old fox. 'I don't think it's possible. But a fox in sheep's clothing! He chuckled. 'That's a good one.'

'I have been watching the birds on a patch of ice in a sheep field not far from here,' said Skulking Dog.

'And what have you learned from that?' asked the old fox.

'I watched many birds feeding on the ice, although what they were eating I do not know. There were wagtails, finches, jackdaws, rooks, magpies, grey crows and gulls, all flocking around the small hollow of ice. Whenever anything approached, the grey crows were the last to go, and when it was gone, they were the first to return. There were also many birds feeding among the sheep, and I was thinking that if I hid in one of the hollows, one of the grey crows might venture too close, or linger too long.'

'Good thinking,' said the old fox. 'And what about lambs?'

'Not a one.'

'Off you go then. And Sinnéad. When he's in place, maybe you could give the crows a nudge in his direction?'

'I too saw many birds,' said Stumpy. 'Beyond the hill man was turning the soil with his machine. Birds of all kinds, including the grey crow, followed him to feed on the worms. I was thinking that since our fur is the same colour as the soil, the birds would not see me and I could feed on them.'

'And while you are watching the grey crow, might not man be watching you?' asked the old fox.

'He has eyes only for the turning soil,' Stumpy assured him.

'Very well then. Perhaps one of you will avenge those of our kind who have lost their eyes to the grey crow. But be careful.'

When they had gone, Old Sage Brush settled down with Scab and Needle Nine and told them stories from long ago. He also told Needle Nine about the Bow in the Cloud, and how it was a sign that somehow the creatures of the earth would survive.

'I knew when I saw the colours of the bow in the river that everything was going to be all right,' said Scab. 'I knew Needle Nine was going to recover.'

Darkness had fallen and the badgers had gone out to grub for worms when the other foxes returned. They brought three members of the crow family with them – a jackdaw, a rook and a magpie. Stumpy's patience in the ploughed field had rewarded him with the jackdaw. From his hiding place in the hollow, Skulking Dog had caught a slightly larger mouthful, a rook, while in the confusion that followed, a magpie had flown into the jaws of his mate. None of them, however, had been able to outwit the grey crow.

'Never mind,' said the old fox, 'you have all done very well. You have brought home food, and you have shown Needle Nine what you can do if you put your mind to it. However, we must also show him that there are sometimes simpler ways of doing things.'

That night they feasted on the cousins of the grey crow, and as they did so, Old Sage Brush told them, 'Fox and crow have always been at odds with one another. The jackdaw is not too bad. But the magpie and the rook, they are alike in many ways. They will betray your presence and steal your food. Even so, we have been able to deal with them. The grey crow is another matter. It goes its own way. It will steal the eye out of your head, but will always be careful to stay well beyond your reach. In such a situation it is not our strength, but its weakness that we must use if we are to deal with it.'

While the others wondered what the weakness of the grey crow might be, he went on the say that according to foxlore their ancestors had faced the same problem, and had solved it very simply. So simply in fact, that the two weakest of the group, Hop-along and Needle Nine would show how it could be done.

'But I have never hunted the grey crow,' protested Needle Nine.

Nor has Hop-along,' said the old fox, 'but he and I have now discussed the matter, and he will show you how.'

At first light, Hop-along and Needle Nine made their way slowly up the side of the valley until they came to a hilltop.

There, far from the eyes of man, and watched only by a few sheep that didn't understand, they preformed a ritual that their ancestors had done many moons before them.

'All you have to do,' said Hop-along, 'is what you did when you first came among us with the choking hedge-trap around you neck.'

'And what was that?' asked Needle Nine.

'Just lie down and let your tongue hang out. Soon the crows will come to feed among the sheep, and as Skulking Dog observed, the grey crows will be the first to venture close. Then, when they think you are dead, they will do what they do when they find a sheep that's fallen on its back and can't get up.'

'What's that?' asked Needle Nine.

'They'll try to peck your eyes out. But unlike the sheep, you'll be able to bite back.

* * *

The river was getting wider now, or as Old Sage Brush would say, a little wiser, tip-toeing quietly around the meadows like an older fox that had learned the value of silence and the need for patience in stalking its prey.

While Sinnéad, for the very best of reasons, had been impatient with her father's reluctance to move on, she now agreed that the rest had given renewed strength not only to Needle Nine, but to those other members of the group, including the old fox himself, who weren't as strong as they might be. The fact that Hop-along and Needle Nine had returned in triumph with a grey crow, had also helped boost the morale of the young fox and was a matter of great rejoicing for all of them.

'It's just that I worry about him,' Sinnéad told Vickey. 'And let's face it, the grey crow could have waited.'

They were lying in the reeds that had now become a feature of the river bank.

Vickey smiled. 'It's only natural that you should worry about him. Just the way She-la worries about Hop-along. But then, perhaps the grey crow was his way of saying that we should slow down.'

Indeed, the more they thought about it, they felt the quest to catch the grey crow was probably the old fox's way of saying a lot of things. They reckoned he was also reminding them that they should do what the river was now doing, take their time, and do what he had always taught them to do: think.

Even now he was lying beside Needle Nine telling him that every step he took must be preceded by a thought, otherwise he would end up with his head in a noose again.

'But how do I learn to do this thinking?' asked Needle Nine.

'The fact that you're thinking about it,' relied the old fox, 'means you've already started!'

'Once,' said Needle Nine, 'I saw a rabbit eating its own droppings, and I remember thinking it must have been as hungry as I was.'

The old fox laughed. 'It is well known among our kind that rabbits do sometimes eat their own droppings, for no animal watches the rabbit more than the fox. But you were lucky to see it. Usually it is only done within the burrow and seen by us when we allow a rabbit to share our earth.'

Had Snout and Sniff been listening, they might well have said that the foxes had only observed such things when badgers occasionally allowed them, and the rabbits to share the many tunnels that formed a sett. However, the badgers were sleeping, as they seemed to do whenever they got the chance, and the old fox continued, 'But why rabbits eat their own droppings is less well known.'

'I thought it was because they were hungry,' said Needle Nine.

The old fox shook his head. 'It cannot be because they are hungry. They eat grass, and goodness knows they do not have to hunt for that. No, in a way I think they are like man's cows.'

'Cows?' asked Needle Nine. 'How can they be like cows?'

'Cows also eat grass,' the old fox told him, 'and it seems to me as I make my way through the fields that they are always chewing it, almost as if it is difficult to digest. Perhaps, and this is only my opinion, the rabbit has the same problem.'

'You mean, it has to eat it twice to get all the good out of it?'

'Exactly. Why else should it do it?'

Needle Nine was thinking of this when Whiskers appeared on the river bank and came over to them. He had an eel in his mouth. It was still curling and squirming, and as he tried to hold it down with his paws, the old fox said, 'You've been in and out of the river a lot today, otter.'

Whiskers succeeded in pinning the eel to the ground. 'Just checking. There's a large lake up ahead, and a dam on the far edge of it.'

'Is that the Edge of the World the others have been telling me about?' asked Needle Nine.

Whiskers shook some drops of water from the hairs on his nose and laughed. 'No. Just the edge of the lake. Like the one in the Land of Sinna, only bigger.'

'But a dam means man,' the old fox reminded him.

'I know,' Whiskers replied. 'But don't worry, I'm checking it out to make sure it's safe to continue.'

'When otters go to the river to hunt,' asked Needle Nine, 'do they have to think?'

'But of course,' said Whiskers. 'We have to think where we are going to find our food, and then we have to catch it. Often we depend on our speed, but we also have our little tricks, just as you have yours.'

Scab, who was lying nearby, came over and lay down beside them. 'You're lucky you don't have to run from the howling dogs like us.'

'Oh but we do,' asserted Whiskers. 'Man sometimes hunts the rivers with howling dogs too, you know. Not the rivers in this part of the country, I might add, but travelling otters have often told me about it. They say it is very difficult to get away from them, especially if you're a female otter.'

'Why is that?' asked Needle Nine.

'Because otters can pup at any time, not like your females who have their cubs in the spring. And if a female is in cub, she has little chance.'

'But you have the river to hide you,' said Scab. 'Man blocks up our earths, and we have to take to the open fields.'

'True,' replied Whiskers, 'but if man hunts when the water is low then there is nowhere to hide.' They watched as he started to munch the eel. 'But even if an otter does survive a hunt,' he continued, 'man and his dogs have trampled all over the river, disrupting the fish and destroying markers that have been built up over many generations, markers that define its territory and contain all the information its family needs to survive.'

'That's dreadful,' said Needle Nine.

'The river,' Whiskers went on, 'is the source of life for us, and for man. Yet man seems to have no respect for it. He will even kill it with the waste from his buildings and his farms.'

'At least you don't have to compete with the stoat when you are hunting,' said Scab.

'The stoat causes us no problem,' Whiskers agreed. 'But more and more we find we are having to share the bounties of the river with the mink and that is something we do not take kindly to.'

While Whiskers had been talking the badgers had joined them, and Snout said, 'I'm glad to say we don't have to think too much about how we are going to get our food. We find all we want in the ground.' He laughed, until his full round belly began to heave, and added, 'But we are always thinking about it!'

Old Sage Brush smiled and said, 'All you have to do is follow your nose. But if Needle Nine here wants to find what is under the ground, he must also listen, or watch the birds.'

'At the Edge of the World,' said Whiskers, 'there are many birds, and they tell me many things, even where the fish are!' One by one the others returned from hunting and as the food was passed around, Whiskers left them to it and disappeared back into the river.

'When will we return from the Edge of the World?' asked Stumpy.

'Why should you think of coming back,' said the old fox, 'when we have not even arrived? The important thing is that we should be out of here before the lambing starts, and better that we should be out of Sheep Land altogether until lambing time is over.'

'I was only wondering how we will know when it is time to come back,' said Stumpy.

Vickey and Sinnéad came over and lay down as they were anxious to hear what the old fox was saying.

'The nights will get short, and the eye of gloomglow will open wide many times before we can return,' Old Sage Brush told them. 'But only when we see the legless ones will we know it is time to go back to the Land of Sinna.'

'You mean the birds with the harsh call?' asked Sinnéad. 'The ones you used to tell us about when we were cubs . . . that lost their legs to man's machines?'

Old Sage Brush smiled. 'Ah, you speak of the birds that used to crake in the corn.' He chuckled. 'When I was young, we used to hear them all the time, and we had great fun trying to find them. You could hear them, but you could not see them. First they would be in one part of the field, then in another, and you had to stop and listen, stop and listen. It was great fun. And you know, they could run very fast.'

He sighed. 'Unfortunately they did not run far enough from man. They stayed in the corn and lost their legs. Then the machines went to the meadows, and they lost their eggs and then they were no more. But no.' He looked up at the sky he could not see. 'It is not the craking birds I speak of, but the ones that are too swift for man to catch.'

'How can that be if they have no legs?' asked Scab.

'The birds in the corn were so used to running they seemed to forget how to use their wings. The birds we must look out for are so used to flying they seem to forget how to use their legs.'

'You mean, they can't walk?' asked Needle Nine.

The old fox nodded. 'Once, when I could see, I saw one landing at the edge of a lake, and it had great difficulty taking off again. It seemed to me its wings were too long and its legs were too short.'

'How do they build their nests then?' asked Stumpy.

'I don't know,' the old fox confessed. 'But they some-times cling to the walls of houses, so maybe they nest up there.'

These were things that even the older foxes had not seen, so they remained silent, determined that when they arrived at the Edge of the World they would keep an eye out for this strange bird.

When Whiskers returned, the old fox said, 'Well otter? What news do you bring this time?'

'Not good,' Whiskers paused to get his breath. 'There's another lake farther on, and another dam. If man started releasing water it could cause the level of the river to rise.'

'Is that a problem?' asked Sinnéad.

'Not for me,' replied Whiskers. 'The more water there is the more I like it. But it could be a problem for some of you.'

Vickey nodded. 'Once, when my cubs were young I took them down to the river below the dam in the Land of Sinna. I had one of She-la's with me too.'

'That's right,' said She-la. 'It was Scab's brother, Scat.'

'The three of them were playing in the river,' Vickey went on. 'Young Black Tip, Little Running Fox and Scat. I was up in the evergreens with my mate, Black Tip when I saw great white streaks on the dam.' She looked at the badgers. 'I remember thinking they were like the stripe on a badger's head. Then I realised man had opened the dam. By the time we got there the river had swollen and the cubs were gone. How they survived, I will never know, but they were like drowned rats when we found them.'

'If it happened here,' said Whiskers, 'I doubt if some of you would survive.'

'Hardly a blind fox,' said Old Sage Brush.

'Or one with three legs,' said Hop–along.

Snout laughed. 'Or a big fat badger.'

The others smiled faintly, and now as they looked at Needle Nine, they knew he couldn't survive such an occurrence either.

'Later,' Vickey continued, and her voice took on a note of deep sadness, 'when the howling dogs were after the cubs, it was Black Tip who ended up in the river. And he wasn't so lucky.'

'Now, now, Vickey,' said the old fox gently. 'I told you Black Tip was able to look after himself.'

'That's right,' said Skulking Dog. 'The fact that he went into the river doesn't mean he didn't come out.'

'And who knows where a dog fox will end up when the urge to find new fields is upon him?' Hop–along told her. 'Especially when he's in the whole of his health.'

Vickey, however, was not to be comforted, and seeing that there was no point in continuing to talk about it, Skulking Dog asked, 'So, what are we going to do? We can't go back.'

'Back?' repeated Whiskers. 'I have no thought of going back.'

'Nor I,' added Old Sage Brush.

'But how can we continue,' asked Scab, 'if we don't have the river to guide us?'

'All rivers lead to the Edge of the World,' Whiskers told him, 'and on my way there, I may follow many of them.'

'So all we have to do is find another river?' said Sinnéad.

'Well, it's not as simple as that,' Whiskers paused, as if wondering how to break the news to them. 'You see, I think we may be on the wrong side of the mountain. The Edge of the World I seek may lie on the other side.'

There was silence as the foxes and badgers thought of what he had just told them, and wondered if it was a journey that might be too much for some of them.

'But when you get there, you will rejoice,' whiskers assured them. 'You will rejoice in a world you have never known, and cannot even imagine.'

'I can imagine it,' said the old fox. 'I can see it all, just as clearly as I can see the Bow in the Cloud.'

The others looked up, but the sky was still cold and clear.

Vickey got to her feet, and going over to the old fox, nudged his grey neck in a way that said she regretted feeling sorry for herself in the company of those who had lost a great deal more than she had.

'We all saw the sign,' she assured him, 'just as clearly as the otter saw it, and if the end of the bow is on the other side of the mountain, then we will find it.'

'But first,' said Whiskers, 'there are many birds on the lake shore . . . and many fish in the lake. You must hunt and I must swim, and, I almost forgot, I found traces of another fox in the woods.'

NINE

By the Light of the Moon

During the night, a sharp frost had descended on the valley to give the evergreens a seasonal touch of white, and the river a ragged edge of ice. The morning air had a crispness that carried sound, and the sounds that reached the ears of the sleeping foxes woke them with a start.

Vickey sprang to her feet, ears twitching to locate the direction from which the sounds were coming. The others were beside her now. 'I thought I heard shots,' she said.

'You did,' Old Sage Brush told her.

Hop-along hobbled over to them. 'Where is it coming from?' They all listened, and knowing how sharp the old fox's hearing was, waited for his reply.

'Sounds plays tricks on you when the air is cold,' he said, 'But I'd say it's coming from the fields above the valley.'

The others nodded, and were wondering what to do when the badgers hurried over to them.

'We thought we heard shooting,' panted Sniff.

'You did,' said Skulking Dog.

'Without an earth we're done for,' said Hop-along. 'The shooters' dogs will surely find us.'

'And us,' said Snout. 'Whatever about you, we'd be like sitting ducks.'

They were all crowding together now, noses in the air, ears twitching to the sound of every muffled shot, the strong wondering about the weak, and none of them knowing whether to run or stay. Then they heard something crashing through the reeds, and fearing it might be a dog, they turned to go.

'Take it easy!' Old Sage Brush urged them. 'That's not a dog you hear. That's the otter.'

The others relaxed, and were relieved when Whiskers galloped up out of the reeds.

'Just as sound can play tricks on you,' said the old fox, so can your imagination. Now calm down, and we will decide what we are going to do.'

'It's the shooting,' She-la told Whiskers. 'It has us a bit on edge.'

'I know. I heard it.' The otter shook himself, and the others wondered how he could fish in the icy water without getting cold.

'What do you think?' Skulking Dog asked him.

'I think you're safe enough.'

'How can you tell?' asked She-la.

'I've been to this lake before,' Whiskers told them. 'It's full of ducks, yet I've never seen any shooters around it.'

Sinnéad, who was standing beside her father, asked him, 'What do you think we should do?'

'We have no choice,' replied the old fox. 'If we continue our journey in daylight, we risk running into the shooters and their dogs. If we continue at night we risk the choking hedge-trays. No, I think it might be safer to stay where we are for the moment.'

'Maybe,' suggested Skulking Dog, 'we could move into deeper cover until the danger passes.'

The old fox nodded. 'Good idea. What do you think Snout?'

The badger looked at his mate, and when Sniff nodded, he said, 'A good deep sett would suit us fine.'

Whiskers laughed. 'There are no setts around here that I've seen, but there is a place, near enough to man, yet far enough away from him where you can hide.'

'All right then, that's settled,' said Old Sage Brush. 'And what about you? What will you do?'

Whiskers smiled. 'I have found a place, not far from the lake, where man is breeding fish. How can I move on until I sample what he has to offer?'

Old Sage Brush nodded. 'And how can we move on until we find the fox that lives by the lake? Skulking Dog, why don't you see if you can find this fox. It may be able to tell us just how safe the area is.'

'Come on then,' said the otter. 'I'll show the rest of you where you can hide.'

As Skulking Dog turned to go, the old fox added, 'And why don't you take Stumpy with you? From what the otter tells me, there are many ducks on the lake, and who knows perhaps we have not tasted all the colours of the bow!'

Stumpy smiled, and dashed off, delighted to be joining Skulking Dog whom he had found to be a very enjoyable and instructive hunting companion. The excitement immediately spread to Scab and Needle Nine, but knowing Needle Nine wasn't yet strong enough to hunt, She-la told them, 'No, not now. Let them check it out first.'

The younger foxes were disappointed, but the vixens smiled at each other, quietly satisfied with the progress Needle Nine was making.

Whiskers led them through woods and reed beds until they came to a place where a smaller river wended its way through a mass of vegetation in such a way that it split here and there to encircle higher ground and form several small islands. The whole area was muddy, but the frost had hardened the mud so that they left no tracks, and no one saw them making their way in through the curtain of vegetation that cloaked one of the islands. No one, that is, except the smallest of birds, for they were now in the hinting ground of the gold-crested wren and the long-tailed tit. Little escaped the notice of the wren which seemed to be everywhere at once, or indeed of the tit as it hung upside down searching for insects in the tangle of lichen-covered branches. However, the foxes knew that unlike the rook or the magpie, these tiny birds would keep quiet and mind their own business.

When they had settled down, Whiskers told them, 'Nearby is a stone bridge, and beyond that there are sheep fields. But beside us is a farm where they breed horses instead of sheep. Somehow I don't think the shooters will want to frighten the horses, so you should be safe here.'

Old Sage Brush smiled. 'Good thinking, otter. And if you spot that fox you were telling us about, you might tell it where we are.'

Whiskers promised he would, but instead of dashing off to hunt, curled up with the rest of them, and they guessed he would wait for darkness before hunting again.

Edging closer on his belly, Needle Nine whispered 'Whiskers?' The otter opened one eye and seeing that he wasn't asleep, Needle Nine went on, 'I was just wondering. What do you do when the river freezes over?'

Whiskers smiled, and realising that the young fox had seen the thin layer of ice forming along the edge of the water, told him, 'The river is like me. It never stops long enough to freeze. But sometimes the lake does.'

'What do the fish do when the ice comes?'

'They move down to the bottom, so I have to hunt in the deeper pools to find them.'

Hearing them, Scab crept over beside them to join in the conversation. 'You said man will kill a river. How can he do that?'

'Man produces much waste besides his own,' Whiskers replied. 'He collects waste from his pigs and spreads it on the fields to make his grass grow. Then he sprays all sorts of things on his crops to make them grow. But sometimes these seep down into the streams and river, and when that happens, they make the weeds grow. The weeds choke the river, and the fish die.'

'That's terrible,' said Scab.

Whiskers nodded. 'But that's not all of it. Where man lives in great numbers, he sometimes dumps the waste from his own body into the river.'

Needle Nine screwed up his nose in disgust. 'You mean he dirties the water with his own waste?'

Again Whiskers nodded, and continued, 'But worst of all, he sometimes pours other things into the river, things that poison the water so that even the weeds cannot grow. When that happens, everything can die, even the river.'

Sniff had also been listening to what the otter was saying, and said, more to herself than anyone else, 'Man has many ways of getting rid of the things he doesn't want, ways you couldn't even imagine.'

The others wondered what she meant, but before they could ask, her mate told her gently to go to sleep.

Scab got to his feet and said to Needle Nine, 'Come on, I'll show you how to fish with your tail.'

'You can't fish with your tail!' replied Needle Nine.

'You can,' Scab assured him. 'Come on. Old Sage Brush showed us how.'

'Be careful you're not seen,' warned She-la, but before she could say anything more, they were gone.

'Don't worry,' Whiskers told her, 'They won't go far. If they catch more than a sliver of ice, they'll be lucky.'

Curious about what Scab had said, Whiskers sidled over to Old Sage Brush, and asked, 'What did he mean?'

The old fox smiled. 'Oh, it's just a little trick I showed him when he was a cub. If we dangle our tail in the river, it seems to attract the minnow. Sometimes they try to pull a hair from it, and if they do, we pull them from the water.'

Snout laughed. 'They'd have a job reaching my tail.'

'Not to worry,' chuckled the old fox, 'you would be a long time getting fat on them.'

Sniff trotted over to She-la and lying down beside her, asked, 'What happened Scab that his fur's like that?'

'He used to have a dreadful itch,' She-la told her. 'Hop-along and I thought he would never survive. He almost scratched himself to death. It nearly drove him mad. Then one day he ran through the fire in the corn stubble. It burned parts of his coat and his skin.'

'But it also burned the mites beneath it,' said Hop-along.

'That's how he survived.' She-la smiled. 'He's not the most beautiful fox in the world but we love him.'

'I'm not surprised,' said Sniff. 'He has great spirit.'

Having failed to find any minnows, Scab and Needle Nine had turned their attention to the narrow frill of thin, clear ice clinging to the edge of the shallow stream that flowed around their island refuge. All it took to break it was the timid touch of a paw, a discovery that soon developed into a race to see which of them could break the most.

Down at the lake, Skulking Dog and Stumpy had found that the ice there had taken a firmer grip. A flock of curlews had found the same, and taken off with plaintive cries to look for an estuary where the mud would be soft and they could search for food with their long curved beaks. Watching them go, the foxes could not know that they too were going to the Edge of the World. In any event, the curlews were quickly forgotten as the two soon discovered, to their amazement, that a great variety of other birds were walking where normally they would be swimming.

The still water in the shallow inlets of the lake had frozen solid, gripping the reeds and grass in a brittle embrace. Coots and waterhens strutted through the frozen grass in a way that clearly showed their discontent, while ducks of every shape and size skidded around on a surface that was too solid for their soft webbed feet.

The lake was ringed by masses of reeds and woods of larch. The trees were bare, and the fluffy heads of the reeds had long since been broken off by the wintry wind, but they gave the foxes all the cover they needed. For once they were on an equal footing with the water birds, and they made the best of it.

Scab and Needle Nine had tired of their game and were enjoying the warmth of their elders when the two hunters returned. They carried two birds each, and the news that more had been stored in the reeds. They also brought the news that there were no choking hedge-traps in the woods, and the vixens immediately raced off to bring back the rest of their catch.

'Any sign of the other fox?' asked Old Sage Brush.

Skulking Dog tore off a leg of duck and pushed it over to him.

'Signs, yes. But that was all.'

'Tell me about the lake,' said the old fox. 'Is it all frozen over?'

'Not all of it,' Stumpy told him. 'Not yet.'

Almost as if he was hearing these words in his sleep, Whiskers awoke to find that darkness was closing in on them. He had been dreaming about the fish that were being farmed in another secluded piece of water, and how he might get through the nets that held them there. Suddenly it occurred to him that if the water froze over, he would never get to them. Jumping to his feet, he raced out through the undergrowth and sped off down the icy stream.

Seeing him go, Needle Nine said, 'If he doesn't get the fish in the nets, he'll have to dive deep.'

She-la shivered. 'I don't know how he does it. I mean, our coats are warm, but I still wouldn't fancy diving into the icy water.'

'It's not the ice he has to worry about,' remarked Old Sage Brush, 'it's the nets.' He paused. 'Now Skulking Dog, what were you saying about the lake? Did you say it wasn't all frozen?'

'Not all of it, but a good bit of it, especially around the edges.'

The moon was now peeping above the horizon, and gradually it pushed the darkness aside to reveal a countryside that was once more white and stiff beneath the frost.

'Where did you find the ducks?' asked the old fox.

'He said they were walking on the ice,' Scab reminded him.

'I meant, where did you catch them?'

'In among the reeds,' Skulking Dog told him.

'I though you said they were standing out on the ice, waiting for you?' said Scab.

'So did I,' added Needle Nine.

'He did,' Sinnéad told them. 'But you can't hunt ducks that are out on the ice. They will go to the edge, and if you follow, the ice might break.'

'They looked tempting, all right,' said Stumpy. 'But Skulking Dog warned me not to follow them.'

'The problem is,' Skulking Dog told them, 'that if the ice breaks and you fall in, it's very difficult to get out. That's why we hunted in around the reeds, where the water was shallow and frozen solid.'

Scab and Needle Nine could see they had a lot to learn, and sensing that they were somewhat crestfallen, Old Sage Brush said, 'Tell me Vickey, what kind of night is it?'

Vickey didn't reply, and realising that she was probably thinking of Black Tip again, Sinnéad told him, 'The wide eye of gloomglow has come up. The sky is twinkling and it's very bright and clear.'

'Vickey,' said the old fox gently. 'You told me before you left that if Black Tip could not be with us, you would be my eyes.'

Vickey got up and went over to him. 'I'm sorry, Sage Brush.'

'I don't want you to be sorry,' he told her, 'especially for yourself. Now, if it's as bright as Sinnéad says it is, why don't you take us down to the lake so that young Scab here and Needle Nine can see the ducks walking on the water?'

Ducks, whether walking or swimming, were of no great interest to the badgers, so they decided to stay in the warmth of their den and sleep. Like man, they would leave this particular night to the frost and the fox.

As far as the foxes were concerned it was an ideal night to go out. Those that could see, could do so perfectly in the light of the moon, and they could see it was a night that belonged to them. This, of course, was something Old Sage Brush could not see, but he could sense it. He could feel the sharpness of the air and the crispness of the grass. He could hear the sounds of happiness as the young foxes frolicked around him, and he knew that somewhere above, the wide eye of gloomglow as watching over them.

Through a gap in the reeds, Scab and Needle Nine looked out in wonder at the gathering of ducks and other birds that seemed to be either sitting or standing on the water.

'What you see on the lake is not real,' the old fox advised them. 'It will disappear beneath you like shifting sand. The reality tonight is what you hear. Listen.'

The two young foxes cocked their heads. Their sharply-pointed ears picked up the sound of an occasional uncertain movement between them and the lake shore, and they realised that in spite of the hunting Skulking Dog and Stumpy had done there earlier, some of the birds had come back in from the lake.

Having indicated that it was now the turn of the younger foxes to hunt, Old Sage Brush followed Skulking Dog and Hop-along down to the lake shore. There they spread out to deter any ducks that might make for the water, while the vixens joined Stumpy, Scab and Needle Nine in hunting among the frozen reeds.

It was a new experience for Scab and Needle Nine to walk on the frozen water, but they soon got the hang of it, and it wasn't long before they were tip-toeing through the reeds as they stalked waterhens, coots and various ducks that had decided to roost there for the night.

It was a game of hide and seek that turned out to be great fun, and highly rewarding. By the time they tired of it, young and old between them had caught more food than they needed, and this they stashed away among the trees.

Hop-along, meantime, had found Whiskers enjoying a game of his own at a place on the lake shore where there was a sloping bank around a shallow inlet. Getting in and out of the water, even with the ice, was no great problem for the otter, and when he then indulged in his favourite pastime of sliding down the bank, he found that the water from his body immediately froze, making his slide even slippier.

Frightened by the activity of the foxes, the waterbirds were now walking around uneasily out near the edge of the ice, the ducks shivering their tails, and the waterhens raising theirs to reveal a white rump that was a sure sign of alarm.

The foxes, however, were no longer interested in them. Their attention was now on the otter and the strange game he was playing. Down he would go and slide across the ice until he came to a stop. Then he would gallop up the far side, race around and throw himself down the slide again.

Curious, Scab went closer to the top of the slide to investigate. His paws immediately lost their grip, and before he knew what was happening, he went whizzing down the slippery path. On reaching the ice below, he tried to get up, but his paws went from under him again, and he spun to a stop with all four legs spread out in a less than graceful landing.

The others laughed, and seeing that Scab was still in one piece, Needle Nine decided to try it. Stumpy followed, and soon the young foxes were eagerly awaiting their turn with Whiskers to go sliding down the bank. Gradually their fur polished the ice below and soon they were trying to see who could go the farthest.

So infectious were their cries of enjoyment, that after a while, Skulking Dog, Sinnéad and She-la also decided to have a go, and then the young foxes were able to laugh at the awkwardness of their elders.

'Why don't you try it, Vickey?' urged the old fox.

Vickey shook her head. 'Someone has to keep an eye out for man, and I don't mind doing it.'

Both the old fox and Hop-along knew she was saying she didn't mind keeping an eye on them. They also knew that wasn't' the real reason why she wasn't joining in the fun, and when at last they decided it was time to return to their den, they weren't surprised to hear her say she would follow them. They realised she wanted to be alone for a while, so they departed from the lake, leaving her to her thoughts, and Whiskers to his game.

Out on the ice, the water fowl continued to shift about nervously, all too aware that one fox and the otter remained. However, they needn't have worried. Whiskers was too busy amusing himself on the slide, while Vickey's thoughts were far away.

TEN

A Cry in the Night

The Great Running Fox in the Sky had started out on its nightly journey some time earlier and was now moving through a mass of twinkling stars. As Vickey lay on the lake shore, she was thinking that on their previous journey with Old Sage Brush they had followed the Great Running Fox. It had been their guiding light until one night, when the clouds had covered it, they had lost their way and strayed into man's place. After that they had relied on Black Tip. He had been a good mate, and had done everything possible to get her back to Beech Paw in time to have her cubs. Later, when the howling dogs had come, he and their dog cub had failed to return and a great light had gone out of her life. Now Young Black Tip was back in Beech Paw, but since leaving there she had been preoccupied with what he had told her. Had Black Tip really been with him? She wondered. Had he really gone back into the river, or was it the young fox's imagination? It was a question that had tormented her so much that she could hardly think of anything else.

A sudden flurry of activity on the ice brought her out of her reverie. Looking around, she saw that Whiskers was no longer sliding down the bank. He had tired of the game himself, and was chasing the water-fowl instead. She watched him running hump-backed across the ice, turning this way and that as the birds skidded and flapped out of his way. Some of them took to the water, where they felt more secure, and in a moment he was gone too, sliding quietly over the edge and into the murky depths.

Despite the cold, Whiskers was now in his element. Speeding up through the lake, he dived under sheets of floating ice and clambered on to others. Where ducks crouched on the ice, he stopped briefly to sport among them, and then he was on his way again, swimming swiftly through a darkened world where the bright light of the moon could not reach. Sometimes he would skim the surface for air, other times he would swirl around the muddy bottom, stirring up fish and other pond life that had sought refuge in the warmer depths among the weeds.

Eventually, guided by one of those animal instincts that man has yet to understand, he emerged from the lake and galloped across the moonlit fields until he came to another lake. This was a small piece of water, sheltered by hills that were covered with patches of evergreens. More important, at least as far as he was concerned, it supported two man-made rafts.

This was the fish farm Whiskers had told his friends about. Anchored in deep water not far from the shore, but just beyond the fringe of ice, the rafts consisted of large rectangular wooden frames. A net of a very fine mesh was slung underneath each of them, and it was in these that brown trout were reared until they were big enough to be released into the local river. Spread over each of the frames was another net to keep birds and other predators away, predators like Whiskers.

In his previous visits to these rafts, or cages as man called them, Whiskers had failed to find a way into the fish. He could see them swimming about in vast numbers, and was greatly frustrated to be so near and yet so far away from them.

Circling them once more, he still couldn't figure out how he might get at them, and finally, in desperation attacked the net hanging beneath one of the cages. Biting and clawing, he did his utmost to break it, only to find that the fine weave held fast. The writhing mass of fish had now begun to flap and splash as they fled to the surface. This excited him even more, and he attacked the net again and again. Still it held fast. He went up for air, and seeing the commotion at the surface lunged at the net in one last desperate effort to break it. Grabbing it with his teeth and claws, he pulled and pushed in a frenzied attempt to tear it apart. What he didn't realise was that in his excitement he was also twisting and turning and when at last he decided to go, he found that the net wouldn't' allow him. It was holding one of his paws just as firmly as it was holding the fish, and he knew he was trapped.

When the water birds had settled down on the ice again, Vickey had turned and headed up the lake, away from the slide where the young foxes had been having such fun, away from the island refuge where young and old now waited for her return. What thoughts drove her to go in the opposite direction, she could not tell. What instinct she followed, she did not know.

Perhaps it was the memory of a mate who had been so dear to her. Perhaps it was the faint scent of another fox. Who can say? But for many hours she made her way through darkened woods and moonlit fields, completely oblivious to any dangers they might hold.

Eventually the soft light of the moon began to give way to the harsh light of day, and she was approaching the top of a small hill when the scream of a fox brought her to an abrupt halt. Looking ahead she saw that she had come to another lake. Almost immediately she heard the scream of the fox again, and quickly spotted it down below her on the lake shore. It was looking out across the ice at several man-made rafts. As she surveyed the scene, she heard another cry, and her muscles gave an involuntary twitch, for she realised it was the squeal of an animal that was trapped.

Although she didn't know it then, Vickey had come to the lake where Whiskers had found the fish farm. She could see the fox and hear the squeals, but from where she was, could not make out what was happening.

Fortunately, Whiskers was near enough the surface of the water to squeeze his nose up between the frame and the net to get some air. He was then able to return to the strands that held his paw and continue to attack them with his sharp front teeth. Time and again he came up for air but as he struggled to free himself, he began to weaken, and he knew it was only a matter of time before he would succumb to the icy water.

The fox that stood on the lake shore also knew from the squeals that were coming from the raft, that the otter would soon exhaust itself, and he had no wish to see it die. He had found that otters often caught more food than they could eat, and what was left over on the river bank sometimes provided him with a convenient meal. For that reason, he had an urge to help it. At the same time he knew that if he went into the water he might not be able to get out because of the ice. There was nothing he could do but stand and scream into the wind.

Looking down at him, Vickey wondered if this was the fox whose traces she and some of the others had found at the larger lake. She could see by the way he ventured out to the edge of the ice and returned that he was uneasy, anxious to go to the creature that was trapped, but afraid to go out too far. Why, she wondered, should he want to go out to it? Surely not for food, not in that icy water. Unless it was some creature he knew, some creature that was useful to him like an otter. An otter!

Vickey immediately thought of Whiskers, and now everything fell in to place. The lake where man was rearing fish. This must be it. And the squeals. Whiskers! It had to be him. He was trapped. But what could she do? Nearby, lights came on and she realised she was beside a big house. Bounding down the hillside, she reached the lake shore just in time to hear a crack and see the ice beginning to break. The other fox clawed to get his footing, but the ice offered no foothold, and she watched in horror as he slid backwards into the water.

Fearing not only for the otter now, but for the other fox, she could only stand, helpless, on the stony shore and cry her alarm into the frozen world around her.

The people in the big house had been awakened by the cries of the first fox. They hadn't paid much attention to it, as they had no hens or other fowl to worry about. Dozing off, they were awakened again. This time they reckoned it was a vixen somewhere down by the lake. They didn't know, of course that there were two foxes involved. Nor were they greatly concerned about it, until the insistence of the cries made them wonder if perhaps something was at the fish cages.

Noting that it was almost morning, the man who looked at the fish dressed hurriedly and went down to his boat. It was in a very sheltered finger of water just below the house, and using an oar to break the thin film of ice that had formed around it, he rowed out into the darkened lake to investigate.

Vickey, who was just around the corner, watched him go. Fortunately, he was not rowing as one would normally row, or he would have been looking back towards the shore. Instead, he was looking ahead, pushing forward on the oars, his eyes focussed firmly on the fish cages. As a result, he was unaware of the drama that was taking place behind him.

Creeping out on the ice as far as she dared, Vickey could see that the other fox was now paddling around in the freezing water. Each time he tried to pull himself out the ice broke, forcing him to paddle round and round again. Realising that if she didn't do something he would soon disappear beneath the water, she urged him, 'Try again. You're nearly there. You've broken off so much ice it must hold.'

The other fox approached the ice again and tried to pull himself out. Once more it broke, and he began to flail the water in a desperate effort to stay afloat.'

'Don't panic,' warned Vickey. 'Take it easy. Try to float. That's it. Once more. Look, the ice is firm. It's holding me.' She squirmed back in case there might be too much weight on it, and watched the other fox place his forepaws on the broken edge. It held firm. She could also see his fur was sodden making him very heavy, and she wondered how long the ice would hold. He inched himself forward and up. She held her breath. He was half way out now. 'Gently,' she whispered. 'That's it. You're nearly there.' He was almost out now. All except his hind legs. 'Keep going,' she urged.

The other fox paused for a moment as if trying to regain his strength, then struggled to get a shivering hind leg up on the ice. At the same time, there was a crack. Scrambling forward on her belly, Vickey caught him by the ear. The ice beneath him collapsed. She held on. For a moment his hind legs pushed the broken ice beneath the surface. She pulled hard, and somehow the extra pull was all that was needed. Almost before she knew it, he was out, lying panting at her feet – wet, cold and exhausted.

Looking down on him, Vickey couldn't help thinking how unlike a fox he was. The wetness of his fur made him look skinny and black and smothered his scent so that she couldn't tell if he was the fox whose faint traces she had found at the other lake.

'Come,' she whispered. 'We must find cover before you freeze.' She glanced back out at the cages. Man was standing on the edge of one of them, plunging a long pole into the water. The squealing had stopped, and she added, 'There's nothing we can do for the otter now.'

In a small patch of evergreens not far from the lake, Vickey watched the man row back to the house. In the way that foxes do, she had licked the life back into the other fox, and left him in the undergrowth to dry. Fearing that Whiskers could not have survived, she returned to the one who had. He was already drying out now, and she found that the fur that had looked so wet and black in the half light of dawn, had turned a handsome russet brown. The tail was also a lovely shade of brown, except for the tip, which was black.

Startled, Vickey took a step back. 'Black Tip?' she ventured, and knowing that occasionally other foxes had a black tip on their tail, she added. 'Black Tip. Is that you?' The scent that was now rising from the other fox was already giving her the answer she so desperately sought.

'Vickey.' The other fox raised his head, and a great feeling of happiness surged through the vixen's mind. It spread through her body and filled her with a warmth she had felt only once before . . . It was a warmth she had first discovered on a wintry hillside back at Beech Paw, a warmth so intense it seemed to match the colours of the bow.

During the day, Vickey lay in the undergrowth with Black Tip, keeping him warm and making him rest until the strength would flow back into his body. Occasionally she heard shots in the distance again. She sat tight and when they didn't come any nearer, she relaxed.

Black Tip was dozing, and as she looked at him, she thought about the first time they had met. It had been a frosty day, just like this one, and she had been wounded by one of the shooters who had come to the meadows below Beech Paw. Black Tip had fought for her then, and she remembered thinking how brave he was. Now, she couldn't help thinking the same. He would probably never admit it, but she had no doubt he had risked his own life down at the lake in an effort to save the otter. Poor Whiskers. The image of the man plunging the pole into the water where he was trapped was clearly etched on her mind and she was greatly saddened by the thought of what had happened to him. Black Tip, of course, didn't know it was Whiskers he was trying to save. He would be very upset to hear it, so she decided not to tell him until he was stronger.

Instead, she told him that their dog cub, Young Black Tip, had survived the howling dogs, and had answered their call to come to the meeting at Beech Paw. Little Running fox was there too, she recalled, and had matured into a beautiful young vixen. She told him about all the foxes and badgers that had been killed and dumped on the bog, and how Old Sage Brush and a few others were following Whiskers to a safe haven at the Edge of the World. Poor Whiskers, she thought again. How were they going to find the Edge of the World now?

When darkness came, and the wide eye of gloom-glow was in the sky, Vickey led Black Tip out of the evergreens and across the fields to the larger lake. From there, they made their way along the lake shore towards the island refuge where the others were waiting.

Vickey, of course, had no way of knowing what had happened to Whiskers. All she knew was that the man had been plunging a pole down into the water where he was trapped, causing her to fear the worst . . .

On reaching the cages, the man had quickly located Whiskers, who was struggling weakly for air between the net and the inside of the frame. It had come as no surprise to him to find an otter there. It had happened before.

At the same time, the net was strong, and he bore no ill-will towards the otter, whose numbers he knew, were few enough.

Going back to the boat, he got a long pole with a hook on the end of it, and began working at the net just below the surface where Whiskers had become entangled. Fortunately, Whiskers was now too exhausted to panic, otherwise he would have frustrated the efforts that were being made to free him.

Wielding the pole almost like a knitting needle, the man worked quietly and patiently, probing the net to try and unravel the strands that held the offending paw so tightly. Now and then he pulled it up as far as he could to help the otter come up for air. It was no longer struggling or squealing and he knew it had tired itself out. At one stage he got a glimpse of a fox up on the hill and thought how well one creature knew when another was in trouble.

By pulling the strands one way and pushing them another, the man gradually managed to loosen them, until eventually only one remained twisted around the paw. Warning the otter of the dire consequences it would face if it dared to come back, he slid the hook underneath the strand and cast it off.

Finding himself free, Whiskers turned and sped away. A short distance from the cage, he came up for air, dived again and circled around to pass the spot where he had been trapped. The net, he could see, had broken where he had been chewing it, and a trout whose curiosity had led it to the opening was poised, wondering what to do. Suddenly it took its chance and made a bid for freedom. Hardly pausing, he caught it, and then he was away.

Not realising that he had lost a fish, the man heaved the damaged part of the net up out of the water, secured it, and climbed back into his boat.

On the frosty shore, Whiskers shook himself vigorously and began munching the brown trout that had almost cost him his life. Occasionally he lifted his head to watch the man's progress as he rowed back towards the house.

Then he forgot about the man and the boat and concentrated on his fish. Suddenly he lost interest in the fish as well, and leaving it half eaten, galloped over the hill.

ELEVEN

Back from the Dead

Having headed straight back to the small island refuge beyond the larger lake, Whiskers was surprised to find that his fox friends were waiting anxiously for Vickey. The last he had seen of her, he told them, was when he had abandoned the slide and taken to the water. But he had heard another fox at the lake with the fish farm.

'It's funny the way it happened,' he told them. 'I got caught in the net, and each time I came up for air, I heard this fox.'

'Are you sure it wasn't Vickey?' asked She-la.

Whiskers shook his head. 'I don't think so. It didn't sound like a vixen.'

'Was it in trouble?' asked Skulking Dog.

'No, but I think it knew I was in trouble.'

'Why, what happened?' asked Hip-along.

'Man came out to see what was wrong. I think he must have been afraid I would break his net and let the fish out. Anyway he worked at it until I was free.'

'And he didn't try to kill you?' asked Stumpy.

Whiskers shook his head. 'No, that was the funny thing about it.'

'There's nothing funny about trying to get yourself killed,' Old Sage Brush told him. 'And what about the fox? What happened to him?'

'I don't know. When I got to the shore there was no sign of him. It was . . . ' He was going to say funny again, but thought better of it, and added, 'It was all very odd.'

'Maybe,' suggested Needle Nine, 'you came across a man who likes otters. I mean, somebody must like them.'

Whiskers smiled. 'If he does, maybe he likes foxes too.'

'I hope so,' said Sinnéad. Like the others, she was concerned that the other fox might have been Vickey, and was worried about the fact that she hadn't returned.

The badgers, who liked to stay together as a family unit, found all this talk of foxes going off on their own and otters diving into icy lakes difficult to comprehend. And so they had listened in a strangely detached way.

Finally, not wishing to appear uninterested or uncon-cerned for Vickey's safety, Sniff said, 'Why don't you follow her scent?'

Knowing that badgers usually confined their outings to short periods around their setts and didn't have the same experience of time and distance as foxes, Sinnéad smiled and told her, 'Her scent will be as cold as the frost now. That's why we couldn't find the other fox.'

The muffled sounds of distant shots came to their ears, and Needle Nine said, 'I hope she's not in any trouble.'

'Vickey was in trouble before she left,' said the old fox. 'Before she left here, before she even left Beech Paw. She has a troubled mind, and until she mends it, she won't be with us either in body or in spirit.'

'What should we do then?' asked Sinnéad.

'Nothing, It's something she has to work out for herself.'

'Maybe we could keep an eye out for her when we go hunting,' suggested Stumpy.

'Of course,' said the old fox. 'But keep out of the sheep fields. And watch out for the shooters. Their shots may be far away, but the danger is always present.'

During the day those foxes that were delegated to hunt did so, far and wide, much wider than they would have admitted to Old Sage Brush. However, the weather continued cold and so did the scents, and as they returned they all brought the same disappointing news that they had found no sign of Vickey. Slowly, very slowly it seemed, the day passed, and as the light faded their fears for her grew. There was little more to be said now, nothing more they could do.

When the moon came up Whiskers slipped back into the river to hunt. Seeing him go, the foxes were tempted to tell him to keep away from the fish farm, but said nothing. They reckoned he had learned his lesson. A short time later the badgers awoke and shuffled off in search of a soft patch under the bushes where they might find some food. Now and then the foxes could hear them clawing down into the softer soil beneath the frosted crust and snuffling around for worms or anything else that might help feed their huge appetites.

'I know they're very good diggers,' She-la whispered to Sinnéad. 'But it must be very difficult for them to find enough. The ground's so hard.'

Sinnéad nodded. 'At least we're catching enough to share with them.'

She-la moved closer as if to share the comfort of a confidence between vixens. 'Sniff never really did tell us what happened to her family. Somehow I think she can't bring herself to talk about it.'

'I noticed that,' said Sinnéad. 'It's almost as if it was too terrible to talk about.'

'She seemed to be saying there are worse things man can do to badgers than anything we've heard about. I wonder what she meant?'

Sinnéad shook her head. 'I just can't imagine. 'She closed her eyes, and before she dozed off, added, 'But she can't keep it choked up inside herself forever. She'll tell us, in her own good time.'

How long they had been asleep, the foxes couldn't tell, but when they awoke, the wide eye of gloomglow was high in the sky, and the badgers were crashing in upon them like the sky itself in a thunderstorm. Thinking something was wrong, they scrambled to their feet, and were ready for flight when Snout told them, 'Vickey! She's back!'

'And there's another fox with her,' exclaimed Sniff.

'Is it really her?' asked Old Sage Brush.

'It's really her,' Sinnéad told him.

'And the other fox?'

Sinnéad paused for a moment, then said, beneath her breath, almost as if she couldn't believe it, 'It's Black Tip.' Realising she wasn't' seeing things, she cried, 'It's Black Tip. It *is* Black Tip.'

In the confusion that followed, it was as if Black Tip and Vickey had found a new family of cubs. So anxious were the others to welcome them back that they almost fell over one another in their efforts to touch noses and renew scents. Like impatient cubs, they also wanted to know where Vickey had been, where she had found Black Tip, where Black Tip had been, and countless other questions.

'Vickey,' whispered the old fox. 'Something tells me you are still unhappy.'

'It's Whiskers,' she replied. 'Black Tip tried to save him, but he was caught in the nets ... At least I think it was him.'

'It *was* him. But don't worry, he didn't drown. He's back,' Old Sage Brush eased himself down, and when Black Tip and Vickey were lying on either side of him, and the others were settled close by, he said, 'Now, enough about the otter. Vickey, how did you find Black Tip? And Black Tip, how did you find your way back from the dead?'

The foxes talked long into the night. Occasionally one of them would look up at the wide eye of gloom-glow and it seemed so happy it occurred to them that it was sharing in their joy. Perhaps, they thought, it was feeling it had played a part in it all, by lighting the way, and who could say it hadn't?

Hop-along edged forward and touched his old friend with the stump of his foreleg, almost as if he wanted to make sure that he was really there. 'We were afraid the howling dogs had claimed you,' he said.

'Not the howling dogs,' Black Tip replied. 'The river. It was the one that almost got me.'

'What happened?' asked Vickey. 'Young Black Tip said he thought you were with him when he went into the river? He also thinks you came back, and that you went into the river again to look for him. What happened? Why did you not return to Beech Paw?'

Skulking Dog had been rooting around for part of a duck he had buried, and when he had given it to Black Tip, he too settled down to hear what his friend had to say.

'I *was* at the river,' Black Tip told them. 'Early on in the hunt, Skulking Dog and I met Young Black Tip. Hop-along and She-la's other cub was there too.'

'Scat,' said Hop-along.

'That's right. We met him and Young Black Tip heading for the earths at Beech Paw. We told them they were all blocked, except the one under the blackthorns.'

'Ours,' said Hop-along.

'Vickey and Sinnéad were with us,' She-la recalled. 'It was the only earth man couldn't get at, because of the thorns.'

'The two cubs decided they would try to keep the howling dogs away from it,' said Skulking Dog. 'And we tried to keep the howling dogs away from them.'

'It worked for a while,' continued Black Tip. 'But not for long. The young dogs gave them a good run, but they were under pressure. They split up, and finally it was Young Black Tip they were after. He kept going as long as he could, and then he came to the river. It was almost dark. His brush was trailing on the ground, and I knew he was nearly finished. I could hear the howling dogs close behind, and was about to try again to draw them off, when I saw he was rooted to the spot. His mind must have been as weary as his body. 'Jump,' I told him. But he didn't move. The only thing I could do was go in with him, and then as I reached the other side I saw him floating down the river.'

Black Tip took another mouthful of the duck. 'The howling dogs had arrived at the other bank at that stage, so I turned and headed off into the trees. I was afraid they would go rooting around after Young Black Tip, and I hoped they would follow me. But they didn't. A short time later I recognised the call of Little Running Fox and guessed she and her friends were also trying to draw them off. That's when I went back to the river. I searched for Young Black Tip, but couldn't find him. Finally, in desperation, I dived in. I don't know how I hoped to find him in there. Maybe I was thinking he might have got snagged on a branch or something, I don't know. But there was no sign of him.

'Before I knew it, I was being swept down the river too. And then I saw his body, lying on a low muddy bank where it had been washed up. I tried to get over to him, but the current swept me past. Suddenly I realised the banks were getting high, and I couldn't get out. The more I struggled, the weaker I got. I couldn't' stay afloat. The river was dragging me down. The river, and the grief, I don't know which was worse. I remember flailing the water and then . . .'

Vickey got up and lay down beside Black Tip, so that he was between her and the old fox. 'And then what?' she said gently.

'I don't know what happened after that. All I remember is finding myself in strange country. I didn't know where I was or what I was doing. I was just wandering. It was like a nightmare. There were rivers, meadows, hills, but I didn't know them. Then one day, it seemed, I woke up to find myself here at this lake. I remembered Young Black Tip, and I remembered you Vickey. I wanted to go back to Beech Paw and tell you what had happened. I didn't know the way, but somehow I felt I could find it. Then one night, when I was watching the Great Running Fox in the Sky, it occurred to me that if I did find my way back it would only break your heart to hear what had happened to Young Black Tip. Better, I thought, that you should think we had both taken off and were still alive, than that you should know one of us was dead.'

'So that's why you didn't come back?' said Vickey. 'You thought Young Black Tip was dead, and you didn't want me to know?'

Black Tip nodded.

'But I knew he was alive,' said Vickey. 'I heard him bark before he took off. What I couldn't understand was why you should take off without saying goodbye. And then, when Young Black Tip told me what had happened at the river, I thought . . . '

'I told you Black Tip was a strong fox and could look after himself,' said Old Sage Brush. 'Now, as soon as the otter returns I think we should push on.'

'I thought you said we shouldn't travel by night in case of the choking hedge-traps?' Sinnéad recalled.

'So I did, but from what the otter tells me, we have to go back up the river for some distance, and we already know the way is clear. Besides that, it is as clear as day, isn't it?

They told him it was and Black Tip said, 'But, are you sure you're strong enough for such a journey? Vickey tells me you have to cross the mountain.'

'We've all had plenty of rest here,' the old fox assured him. 'And plenty to eat. We're as fit as we'll ever be.'

'But why don't you stay here until the lambing season is over?' asked Black Tip. 'It's safe. And as you say, there's plenty to eat.'

The old fox smiled, and placing a paw on Black Tip's said, 'Because this is only the edge of the lake, and we are going to the Edge of the World.'

'But why should you want to go to the Edge of the World?' asked Black Tip. 'I don't understand.'

'That's because you haven't heard the otter,' said the old fox. 'And I would rather you heard it from him.'

While the arrival of Black Tip and Needle Nine was a matter of great rejoicing, their presence created a problem. Old Sage Brush, of course, was too polite to put it that way, he merely pointed out what must have been obvious to those who could see. This was that there were now too many of them to travel together in one group, and that they must split up. So it was that Black Tip and Vickey took the lead. She-la followed with Old Sage Brush, Hop-along and the younger foxes. The badgers came next, and Skulking Dog and Sinnéad brought up the rear. As for Whiskers, he continued to pop in and out of the river and in and out of whatever group took his fancy. Later, when it came to finding the river that would lead them to the Edge of the World, he would show them the way.

They made good progress, and when dawn arrived they rested up in a tangle of undergrowth that grew in a rocky clearing in the middle of a patch of evergreens. During the day those that could hunt did so, and they brought back enough food for everyone.

It was evening by the time Skulking Dog and Sinnéad returned, and they also brought the news that on a remote farm they had come across a badger sett. It was news that immediately awoke Snout and Sniff from their slumbers, and they eagerly inquired if the sett was occupied.

'It seems to be,' Sinnéad told them. 'We didn't delay too long at it, mind you. It's too near the house. But I'd say there are badgers in it all right.'

'How near is it?' asked Snout. 'I mean to the house?'

'It's at the top of a steep bank at the back of the house. The entrance is in under the hedge where man won't see it if he looks up, but I'm sure he must know it's there.'

'Maybe,' said Whiskers,' man doesn't mind it being there. I mean, it does happen. Look what happened to me at the fish farm. Who would have thought man would let me go?'

Vickey was tempted to say the otter had almost got Black Tip and himself drowned over his foolishness, but restrained herself when she saw the sow badger sniffing in a way that indicated she was going to say something.

'Are there any cattle on the farm?' Sniff asked.

'There are some all right,' Skulking Dog told her. 'And pigs. Man has been spreading the pig waste on his fields.'

'It's all over the place,' said Sinnéad. 'It's horrible.'

'If there are badgers in the sett, I'd love to go and see them,' said Sniff. 'It's so long since I've spoken to any of our own kind.'

'Then why don't you?' asked Sinnead.

Sniff looked up at the moon so that its light reflected in her eyes, and the foxes couldn't help noticing once again how small and white they appeared to be. 'Our eyes aren't much good to us,' she told them. 'We spend too much time under the ground. All we can see is the general outline of things, no detail. That's why we don't normally stray far from our sett.'

'So you see,' added Snout, 'we'd never find it.'

'But you don't have to,' said Sinnéad. 'We'll take you.'

'No,' Sniff hesitated. 'We . . . we couldn't.'

'Of course you could,' said Old Sage Brush. 'Why don't you both go? Sinnéad and Skulking Dog will make sure you set there, and back.'

'That's right,' said Skulking Dog. 'There are no choking hedge-traps between here and there that we could see, so it should be safe enough to travel by dark.'

'We wouldn't want to delay you,' said Snout. 'But perhaps we should warn. Tell them what happened to us.'

Good idea,' said the old fox. 'The Edge of the World can wait. We all have our worlds, and it appears to me your friends are on the edge of theirs.'

Skulking Dog and Sinnéad were surprised how quickly the badgers could run when they didn't have to stop and sniff their way around. Their legs were short, and their bodies wide and fat, but they were very muscular, and their hair bounced upon their flabby bodies as they lurched across the moonlit countryside. Now and then the foxes stopped to allow them to get their breath, then they were off again, and before the darkness had completely lifted from the land, they arrived at the farm.

Hardly stopping to say goodbye, the badgers disappeared into the sett. Peering through the hedge, Skulking Dog and Sinnéad found themselves looking across at a window of the farmhouse. From the direction of the yard they could hear pigs squealing and grunting, but it was the window that held their attention. It was lit by something similar to the eye of gloomglow, and they could see a man spreading something on his chin with a small brush. Furthermore, when he rinsed the brush in a mug, they could see its hairs were black and white.

'He's rubbing his chin with badger hairs!' Skulking Dog exclaimed.

Fascinated, they watched man go through this old-fashioned form of shaving, and when they realised what he was doing, they had to laugh.

'So that's what Sniff was talking about,' said Sinnéad. 'Man rally does use badger fur to get rid of his own!'

Snout came bouncing back up out of the sett. 'It's occupied all right,' he told them.

'They're mad to make a home here,' said Skulking Dog. 'Just beside man. And look. He's using badger fur to rub the fur from his face.'

Snout looked, but couldn't see. 'They're a young pair of badgers,' he continued. 'The sett was empty when they found it, so they just moved in. We're trying to get them to move somewhere safer.'

'Good idea,' said Sinnéad. 'I wouldn't fancy trying to find food around here, not with all this pig waste on the grass. It smells awful.'

'We'll go and hunt now,' Skulking Dog told him. 'If you can get your friends to move, wait until dark. We'll come again just after dusk, and as soon as they're settled somewhere else, we'll take you back.'

'Thanks,' said Snout and immediately flung his great bulk back down into the sett.

Relieved to be leaving the slurry-sodden fields, Skulking Dog and Sinnéad hurried away. Taking care to avoid any sheep that were in the area, they hunted until they were full and lay up for the rest of the day on a rocky hillside where they could keep an eye out for danger. They were anxious to give Snout and Sniff as much time as possible with their friends and didn't leave for the pig farm until well after dark. When, eventually, they did arrive at the sett, they found to their dismay that man had been there before them. During the day he had brought his machine back to the field, and having blocked all ways of escape, had pumped slurry into the sett until it was brimming over. Man, as Sniff had said, had many ways of getting rid of things he didn't want, and now she herself had fallen victim to one of them.

TWELVE

A Close Shave

Beneath long red briars that spanned the world where they lay like the Bow in the Cloud, the other foxes curled up and talked about things that were far beyond their understanding.

Because of their activities in the area rabbits were becoming scarce and harder to catch. During the day they had hunted with only limited success and as there were many mouths to feed, they decided that after dark when the rats of the river bank came out, they would venture forth again.

In the meantime, they talked about Ratwiddle. Vickey told Black Tip about Ratwiddle's dream, and now he wondered, as indeed they all did, what he meant.

'Do you think he was dreaming about he future?' asked Vickey. 'Or the past?'

'What did he say again?' asked Black Tip.

'He said he had seen the rats hunting the fox,' Hop-along recalled.

Remembering how Old Sage Brush had rebuked them for giggling at Ratwiddle under Beech Paw, the younger foxes were afraid they might say the wrong thing, and remained silent.

'Well, many the bite he has got from them,' said Black Tip. 'That's what has him the way he is. But . . . he also has a strange way of dreaming about the future. What do you think, Sage Brush?'

'I think he *was* dreaming about the future,' replied the old fox. 'Maybe even trying to warn us of some of the dangers we may face. You see, he may have been bitten by rats in the past, but where would he have seen man walk upon the water as he hunts for fish? Or a great green caterpillar in the sky hunting for man? None of us has ever seen anything like that in our travels, not even Ratwiddle.

'Do you think we should be carefully then?' asked She-la, 'Even on the river bank?'

'We must go carefully wherever we go,' the old fox told her, and knowing her concern was not for herself, but for Scab, he added, 'That's not to say that any of us, even our youngest, should leave the river bank to the rat. As far as the rat s concerned, we are the hunters, not the hunted.'

No creature, or course, knew more about the river bank than Whiskers. He knew the places beneath it where the rats had their holes, the paths they took when they left them and the points at which they were likely to cross the river. It was with obvious pleasure, and indeed considerable pride, that he showed his friends all of these things. Then, leaving them to catch the rats for themselves he went off down the river to hunt for something more to his own liking.

Later when the sound of a creature running came to the ears of the foxes, they thought it was the otter returning. To their surprise, they found it was Sinnéad. She was alone and out of breath, and the very fact that she had abandoned some of her usual caution in her anxiety to reach them, told them something was wrong.

When they heard what had happened, Scab asked, 'But how could man do that to them?'

'Man does many things we cannot understand,' Old Sage Brush told him. 'We kill for food. He sometimes kills just to get rid of us. That's why he left so many of our kind on the bog. He didn't want us for food, and he didn't want us for fur.'

'He nearly killed me,' Stumpy recalled, 'and all he wanted was my tail.'

'But to flood the sett with pig waste.' Needle Nine screwed up his nose in disgust. 'That's a dreadful thing to do.'

'No worse than what he did to you,' She-la told him.

'At least I could breathe,' said Needle Nine,' which is more than Snout and Sniff can do.'

'But are you sure they were in the sett?' asked Black Tip.

Sinnéad nodded. 'That's where we left them, and it's hardly likely they would have come out during the day.'

The others knew this to be true, and as they reflected on the tragedy of it, Sinnéad told Black Tip, 'Skulking Dog wants you to come back with me.'

'What for?' asked Hop-along. 'No one can help them now.'

Sinnéad shrugged. 'I know, but maybe he thought we could nose around, just in case.'

Black Tip nodded. 'Good idea.'

'I'll go too,' said Vickey. 'With all that pig waste around, you might need an extra nose.'

Before any of the others could offer to go, Black Tip told them, 'Right. But the rest of you sit tight.'

'We'll be here,' said the old fox. 'And don't worry about us. There's safety in numbers. But you be careful, all of you. There can be danger in numbers too, especially on a farm like that where strong smells dull the scent and cloud the mind of man.

As soon as Sinnéad had gone for help, Skulking Dog had searched the surrounding fields in case Snout or Sniff or any of the other badgers had been out of the sett when man had come to flood it. He saw no sign of them, and as the pig waste on the grass prevented him from finding any scents, he headed for an overgrown mound in the middle of one of the fields.

The mound had been formed when man had cleared rocks, tree stumps and other debris from the field and heaped them around a clump of trees. There were several of these mounds on the farm, and Skulking Dog had arranged to meet Sinnéad and Black Tip at the one nearest the badger sett.

Squeezing in under a tree stump that was now the host to moss and various fungi, he found that a badger had got there before him. It had pushed in as far as it could in its efforts to get away from something. Skulking Dog knew before ever he saw the face of the heaving body, that it was Snout, for he knew from the way it was heaving and the sobbing that came from the hidden head, that it was consumed with grief.

Speaking quietly, he consoled Snout as best he could, and eventually persuaded him to turn around and talk to him.

'First our cubs,' said Snout, 'and now Sniff. What did we do to deserve this?'

''Are you sure she's in the sett?' asked Skulking Dog.

Snout nodded. 'After you left us we stayed up most of the day talking. We were so excited to see each other, we forgot to sleep. We had a lot to talk about, especially Sniff and the other sow. Eventually I drifted off. When I awoke the other sow was telling Sniff about life in the sett where she had been reared. Her mate had fallen asleep too, but with all this travelling by day when I should be sleeping and sleeping at night when I should be eating, my whole routine is upset. I was hungry, so I decided to go out and find something to eat. It was still daylight and I was grubbing around in one of these mounds when I heard man taking his machine into the field where the sett is. I had to lie low and wait until he left. I thought he was just spreading more pig waste on the grass. It never occurred to me that he was . . . ' Snout began to sob again. 'He just poured it in on top of them. It was horrible.'

'I know,' said Skulking Dog gently. 'We saw it when we came to take you back.'

'There was nothing I could do about it,' Snout sobbed. 'All the exits were packed tightly with stones and earth. I tried, but here was nothing I could do.'

'Sinnéad has gone for Black Tip,' Skulking Dog told him. 'Maybe we can do something to help.'

Snout lowered his head and his huge body began to heave again. 'They're in the other world now,' he said. 'There's nothing anyone can do to help them.'

Skulking Dog did his best to comfort Snout, but the badger was not to be consoled, and even the arrival of Sinnéad and her two friends failed to rouse him from his grief.

'What do you think?' asked Black Tip. 'Is there any possibility they could still be alive?'

'I don't see how,' Skulking Dog whispered. 'The sett was full to the brim.'

They were standing at the edge of the mound, and could hear the vixens trying to coax Snout out from under the tree stump.

'Did you hear any movement?' asked Black Tip. 'Anything at all?'

Skulking Dog shook his head. 'All we could hear was the squealing of the pigs.'

Black Tip cocked an ear in the direction of the farm. 'They're quieter now. Maybe we should go back and listen again.'

Skulking Dog nodded. 'Why not? Come on, I'll show you where it is.'

The vixens agreed to keep an eye on snout, and the two of them set off across the darkened fields.

When the farm buildings loomed up ahead, Black Tip suggested that they check first to see if there were any dogs.

Splitting up, they loped over the low concrete walls that divided various parts of the yard, and stole quietly in around the out-houses. The smell of pigs and their waste was even stronger in the yard, but they reckoned dogs would sense their presence, even if they couldn't smell them. As it happened, the farmer had little use for dogs since he had only a few cattle, and the absence of barking told them the way was clear to go up and check the sett.

The lights had gone out in man's house, and only the occasional squeal from the pig houses disturbed the stillness of the night. Skulking Dog showed Black Tip the flooded sett, and when they had carefully examined it, Black tip lowered his head so that he could listen close to the ground and told his friend to do likewise. This was something Skulking Dog and Sinnéad, shocked by what they had found, had not thought of doing. Not that it would have done any good because of the noise the pigs were making at the time.

Now if a mouse moved, Black Tip and Skulking Dog would hear it, and as they cocked their sensitive ears this way and that, they did hear something – not a mouse scurrying about beneath them, but a snuffling noise.

'There it is again,' whispered Black Tip. 'Do you hear it?'

Skulking Dog lowered his head farther and listened intently. After a moment or two he nodded, saying, 'What do you think?'

'It could be a rabbit that's trapped somewhere in the sett. Or it could be the badgers.'

'Do you think maybe they've managed to keep their heads above the pig waste?'

Black Tip shook his head. 'I don't know. But there's something moving down there. Let's go back and ask Snout.'

The vixens still hadn't succeeded in snapping Snout out of his grief, but the news that the two dog foxes had heard movement in the sett, did. He immediately scrambled back out from under the tree stump and galloped off. The foxes hurried after him, and it was only when he slowed down to find a way through a hedge that they succeeded in stopping him.

'Take it easy,' Vickey urged him.

Snout ignored her and was looking desperately for a way through the hedge when Black Tip warned him. 'If they are alive, they won't be for long, not if you go on like that.'

Snout stopped and asked, 'But I must get to them. I must help them.'

'If you go crashing in like that you'll only get yourself killed,' said Black Tip, 'and we need you.'

He could see from the way Snout was looking at him with his glassy eyes that he didn't understand, and added, 'We need you to do the digging. It all depends on you.'

Gradually Snout calmed himself. 'I'm sorry,' he said. 'I don't know what I'm doing. It's just the thought of Sniff and the others being in there . . . I . . . I . . . '

'We know,' said Sinnéad gently, 'But if they are alive, and if there is any hope of getting them out, we'll have to go about it with great caution. The sett is very near the house, and if man hears us, that'll be the end of it.'

Snout nodded. 'All right. What do you want me to do?'

'We've checked out the farm buildings,' said Skulking Dog, 'and as far as we can see, there are no dogs around. Just follow us, and maybe we can figure out something.

In the darkness of a sett, sight is of little use to badgers. Touch, hearing and smell are their most important senses. Now, hearing was the only sense that was of any use to Snout, and even that was not as acute as the hearing of the foxes.

'Are you sure you heard something?' he asked anxiously.

'I can hear it,' said Sinnéad. 'Listen.'

The others confirmed that there were sounds of some sort coming from the sett, and Snout, who thought he too could hear something now, asked, 'But how are we going to get down into it?'

'We can't get down into it,' Black Tip told him, 'but perhaps we can get up into it.'

'I don't understand,' said Snout.

'We can't get down through the pig waste,' Black Tip explained. 'But if we dig up into the embankment, we might be able to let it out.'

'That's a great idea,' said Skulking Dog.

'What if man hears us?' asked Sinnéad. 'We saw him the first time we came here. He's just opposite us.'

'Man's asleep,' replied Black Tip. 'If he can sleep through the squealing of pigs, perhaps he can sleep through the noise of our digging.'

The problem was, where to start digging? If they succeeded in letting the pig waste out of one chamber, it might still remain in the rest of the sett.

'Snout,' said Vickey. 'Sinnéad told me you were in the sett. If they're still alive, where do you think they're likely to be?'

Snout looked at the uneven outline of the embankment, and thought of the sleepy day he had spent inside it with Sniff.

'There's one chamber that might be higher than the rest,' he recalled. 'Maybe they took refuge in that. I think it's higher. I'm not sure.'

'Well, we can only do our best,' said Black Tip. 'Let's dig.'

Snout indicated the spot on the far side of the embankment where they should start, and anxious to show his support for what he had proposed, Black Tip started to dig. First the grass began to fly, then the soil and pebbles. Some of these hit the door of the house below, and almost immediately a light came on in the window opposite. Hurriedly they scrambled out of the ray of brightness and watched from the shadows as man peered out. Fortunately there was little for him to see, and soon they were in darkness again.

'Better leave the digging to me,' suggested Snout, and from the cover of the hedge they watched as he began raking the embankment with rapid strokes of his powerful claws. His broad body, they could see, prevented the soil from hitting the door. As a result it collected under him. Every now and then he arched his body and brought his back legs up to push it behind him. Some of the soil and stones trickled down the slope, but didn't make too much noise. Soon he had disappeared from their view, and all they could see was the loose earth being pushed back out of the tunnel.

Up and up Snout burrowed, stopping occasionally to come out and look up towards the hedge, presumably to make sure he was still going in the right direction. On these occasions, the foxes offered to take over so that he could rest, but he would have none of it. With a snort and a snuffle that stopped short of a sneeze, he cleared the soil from his nose, and dived back into the ever-lengthening tunnel.

Time passed and the foxes watched and waited. Their thoughts switched back and forth, from the three striped snouts that might be gasping for air not far below them, to fears that man might discover what they were doing. In between they couldn't but admire the skill with which Snout removed the soil that had gathered behind him. Moving backwards in a series of jerks, he pushed the soil out with his bottom, at the same time dragging more between his forelegs and body.

They were, they realised, watching a master digger at work. Bit by bit the mound at the entrance to the tunnel took on a familiar shape, spreading up and out as it did at the entrance to all badger setts. Slowly, almost imperceptibly, the mound grew until the loose stones that trickled down, started to roll across the concrete path. So gradually did this occur, and so gently at first, that none of the foxes noticed the danger. It was only when the stones began to rattle on the bottom of the door like a shower of hail stones, that they realised what was happening.

Suddenly the light came on in the house again and it was obvious to the foxes that this time man had seen what was happening. Hurrying down to the entrance of the tunnel, Black Tip dashed inside to warn Snout.

'I can't stop now,' the badger panted. 'I'm nearly there.'

'Man has seen us.' Black Tip told him. 'Hurry. You must get away.'

Ignoring him, Snout clawed desperately at the thin wall of earth he knew separated him from the sett.

Turning, Black Tip raced back out. Lights had now come on around the door of the house. Above him he could hear Vickey calling, urging him to hurry. With one last look back at the tunnel, he bounded up the slope and took cover behind the hedge. The others were on their feet, ready to go. Below them they saw the door opening and a man framed in a beam of yellow light. He was fumbling to load his shotgun, and while they did not know what he was doing, they could see from what he was carrying that he was a shooter.

Hearing a rumbling noise directly under them, they switched their gaze to the tunnel entrance. To their surprise they saw Snout flinging himself out, closely followed by a torrent of pig waste. As Snout scrambled back up to the hedge, the liquid manure spewed out and upwards, arching across the narrow space between the embankment and the house. It hit the man in the chest, and as he struggled to get away from it, he slipped and landed on his back.

After a few moments the torrent of manure eased off, and sliding down out of the tunnel came three bedraggled badgers. Unable to stop, they slid right down to the bottom of the bank and came to rest at the man's feet. There they picked themselves up, and skidding in their anxiety to get away, sprayed him with another shower of manure.

Behind the hedge, the foxes smiled, but then to their horror, they saw the man scrambling to his feet and taking aim. Two thunderous shots rang out, flame belched from the muzzle of the gun, and clusters of deadly pellets tore into the escaping badgers. Two stopped in their tracks, rolled back down the embankment and lay still. The third reached the hedge and safety.

In the darkness of the other side, Snout whispered, 'Sniff is that you?'

The escaping badger gave a quick nod, and looking anxiously around asked, 'But what about the others?'

Before Snout or the foxes could reply, another shot rang out and the pellets ripped through the hedge above them. Taking off across the fields, they didn't stop until they had left the farm far behind, and only then to enable Sniff to get her breath back. Glancing around, she waited for a moment in the forlorn hope that the friends she had known so briefly might come bounding after her. She hadn't seen them falling back down the slope, and the others didn't have the heart to tell her. There was no movement in the shadows, and somehow she sensed they wouldn't be coming. Sobbing bitterly, she turned to Snout, and together they took off into the darkness.

THIRTEEN

Over the Top

During the night snow fell on the mountains and their peaks were white and bright against the early morning sky. From the wooden rail of a remote hillside sheep paddock, three grey crows watched the strange procession of creatures, that made their way up through the heather towards them. Like the foxes and their friends, the grey crows had forsaken the valley, leaving it to the rooks. The lambs were getting stronger now, too strong even for the grey crows, and the rooks had come to the sheep fields to squabble over the lambs' droppings which were highly nutritious with their mother's milk.

Following her rescue, Sniff washed herself to get rid of the stench she would forever associate with death, and with Snout's help spent the remaining hours of darkness grooming herself until the smell of pigs had gone and the familiar scent of her mate returned. Then, in the early dawn, with only mountain sheep and hungry crows to see them, they wended their way up through the rushes and under the heather, following Whiskers in a search for the river he knew lay some-where on the other side.

The snow, which, from a distance, appeared to cover the mountain tops, was in reality quite light. More severe was the overnight frost, but the morning sun was already releasing the bog water from its icy grip so that it was beginning to seep beneath the moss once more. Where previously it had dripped down bare mud banks and frozen, icicles had formed, hanging like fangs from the overhanging grass. Now as the creatures of the lowlands passed, these were slowly melting in the sun, swinging in the wind and jangling together in a strangely rigid refrain. Occasionally one came crashing on to the icy humps below, causing the foxes to jump aside in momentary fright. Otherwise, nothing deflected them from their path and they trotted on with great deter-mination, picking their way through rocky streams and peaty crevices until they came to the top of the mountain.

Whiskers paused as if to decide which way to go, and they wondered what instinct he was acting on when he nodded, and said, 'This is the way all right.'

They watched as he scouted around the hummocks and heather, sniffing at dark peaty pools. Up here, the brown, lifeless water was still frozen over, and all he found was an empty beer can, held by the ice long after man had dropped it from his hand. There was no sign of man himself, and seeing that Old Sage Brush and Hop-along were tired after the long climb, the vixens suggested they rest for a while.

A discarded fridge also lay in the heather, demon-strating man's disregard even for the remotest part of his environment, and they followed the sheep paths until they came to a place where no sign of human activity was to be found. There they settled down in a clump of withered ferns and with nothing to disturb them but the sound of the wind in the rushes, some of them slept while others talked or took stock of their new surroundings.

Leaving the vixens to talk among themselves, Black Tip went over to the badgers. They were lying beside Old Sage Brush and Hop-along, both of whom were dozing. He was reluctant to talk about what had happened back at the pig farm, but felt he owed it to the badgers to say something. 'I'm sorry my plan didn't work out,' he told them.

'I'm glad it worked as well as it did,' Snout replied. 'At least we got Sniff out.'

Black Tip lowered his head and looked at Sniff. 'I didn't count on your two friends getting killed.'

'That wasn't' your fault,' Sniff assured him. 'That was man's doing.' She sniffed to hold back a tear. 'But why? That's what I can't understand. I mean, what harm were they doing?'

Black Tip shook his head. 'None at all.'

Hop-along opened his eyes. 'Maybe he didn't like them living so near to him.'

'But why?' said Snout. 'They weren't going to bite him.'

'And it wasn't' as if they were going to harm his pigs,' added Sniff.

Old Sage Brush was wide awake now too. 'You might as well say, why does man kill a river? Maybe he doesn't see any use for it. Or maybe it's just because it's there.'

'Do you really think man will be friendlier at the Edge of the World?' asked Snout.

'Well,' said the old fox, 'he can't be any worse, and if Whiskers is right, he might be a lot better.'

The vixens were watching the three younger foxes exploring the maze of paths and scents that were to be found beneath the heather.

'Needle Nine has come on well,' observed Vickey.

She-la nodded. 'He seems to have completely recovered. You can hardly see the mark on his neck now.'

'I wonder if they'll find any young vixens at the Edge of the World?' wondered Sinnéad. 'It's coming near that time.'

The other two smiled, and Vickey said, 'Who knows? If Whiskers can find the answer to his dreams there, why can't they?'

Skulking Dog had gone off on a more serious quest than the younger foxes, and now returned to say that food was scarce on the mountain.

'Not even a snipe,' he reported, adding, 'Not that we could catch them anyway.'

Snout, who was nibbling through Sniff's fur to help restore it to its original condition, stopped and said. 'The snipe can't feed when the frost hides the worms. I think they've gone down to where the mud is softer, and maybe we should do the same.'

Old Sage Brush lifted his head. 'That's the best suggestion I've heard today.'

Sinnéad, concerned as always for her father's well-being, went over to enquire, 'But have you rested enough?'

'I'm fine now,' he assured her. 'How about you Hop-along?'

Hop-along hobbled to his feet. 'I'm okay. Anyway, it's all down hill now as far as I can see.'

'What do you see?' asked the old fox

'Heather, valleys, patches of evergreens.'

'As far as the eye can see,' added Vickey.

'With your eyes,' Whiskers told them, 'you may soon be able to see the Edge of the World.'

'I can see it already,' said Old Sage Brush. 'I suppose that's one advantage of being blind. But Snout's right. If the snipe are feeding lower down, so are other birds. And if they eat, so do we.'

Man was nowhere to be seen on the mountain. Even his sheep seemed to be left to do as they pleased. They nibbled and watched, and what they saw they could not comprehend. They moved aside to allow the strange collection of migrants to pass, and soon forgot they had ever seen them.

It was a new experience for the foxes and badgers to be able to move without fear of man, and they made good progress. In addition to patches of evergreens, they came across occasional small groves of mountain ash and birch. The berries had gone from the mountain ash, but as Sinnéad observed, it was coming near the time of year when the earth would begin to renew itself. That was a time, the older ones knew, when the leaves would grow and the birds would sing, and the young foxes would discover their place in the unending cycle of life.

In the meantime, there was food to be found, and when they finally came to a halt beneath the familiar white bark of the birch, it was the pains of hunger that sent forth the hunters, not the bidding of Old Sage Brush.

The cool clear water of a stream that came to the surface from a secret spring within the mountain trickled through the birch grove giving the ground a green growth which other parts of the mountain did not have. It also gave the mud a richness which was not to be found on the higher reaches of the mountain, and here the two badgers were able to grub for worms to their hearts' content. The stream itself was the food of life for Whiskers, and he set off to explore it with the enthusiasm of a fish that has just been returned to the water.

It was the young foxes who came back first. Stumpy had caught a red grouse, and the other two were beaming with pride, as they considered that they had helped him find it. The fact was that Scab and Needle Nine had followed a scent that had led them to one of the smallest of birds. They had wasted a lot of time chasing a family of wrens through the heather, but that's not to say they weren't on hand when Stumpy caught the bigger bird, and so they shared in his moment of pride. Some of the older foxes also returned with grouse, and as they enjoyed their first full meal for some time, Vickey observed that Black Tip was very quiet.

'It's . . . It's nothing.' He shrugged. 'Nothing really.'

Old Sage Brush, who could tell more from silence than anyone else, said, 'That means it's something. Tell us what did you see?'

Black Tip hesitated. 'You'll think the river has softened my brain.'

'No we won't,' Vickey assured him. 'What did you see?'

Black Tip licked his lips and said, 'I saw a cow. Or at least I think it was a cow.'

'What's so strange about that?' asked Hop-along.

Black Tip looked around him, as if daring them to laugh. 'It had a tree growing out of its head.'

Scab lowered his nose and sniggered, and Needle Nine nearly choked on a piece of grouse. Even Old Sage Brush had to smile. 'A cow with a tree growing out of its head. Well, that's something even I have never seen.'

Skulking Dog was trying not to laugh. 'What sort of tree was it?'

They all started to laugh now, and Black Tip said to Vickey, 'There, I knew they would laugh.'

'I'm not laughing,' said Vickey. 'Do you mean it had some kind of horns?'

'I suppose so. But they weren't like any horns I've ever seen before. They were more like the branches of a tree!'

'Sometimes sheep have very curly horns,' said Hop-along. 'Were they like that?'

'Or like the horns of a goat?' suggested Skulking Dog.

Black Tip shook his head. 'These were big horns, with many branches on them, just like a tree.'

'And what about the tail?' asked Stumpy. 'Had it a tail like a cow?'

'That's another funny thing,' Black Tip told them, 'It had a short tail, like a rabbit.'

The three younger foxes could no longer contain themselves. Scab sniggered. Then Needle Nine. Somehow it was contagious. Stumpy tried to suppress a snigger, but couldn't. Scab and Needle Nine laughed at him, and suddenly they were all laughing.

She-la admonished Scab and told him to go off and do something useful, like catching a grouse. All three took her advice and made themselves scarce.

'You can laugh if you like,' said Black Tip when they had gone. 'But I did see it. And it didn't look as funny as it sounds. It was a fine, proud looking animal that kept its head high and its nose to the wind. It had a mane too . . . '

'You mean like a horse?' asked Hop-along.

'Not really. It was under its neck. I know, it sounds ridiculous, but maybe you'll see it yourselves.'

Strangely enough, it was the one who could never see such a thing who didn't doubt what Black Tip had told them. Old Sage Brush tried to imagine this strange creature, but couldn't. However, he reminded the others that once, when they had strayed into man's place, they had told him about the strange creatures they had seen, animals with noses so long they reached to the ground, others with necks so high they fed on the tree-tops, giant mice that carried their young in pouches on their bellies, even giant ginger cats.

This, the others had to admit, was perfectly true. At the same time, some of them couldn't help wondering if perhaps, Black Tip's brain had been addled by his long immersion in the river, and he was now having the sort of strange visions that tormented poor Ratwiddle's mind.

Vickey had no such doubts. She knew Black Tip longer than any of them, and she knew that if he said he had seen a cow with a tree growing out of its head, then he had seen it. She also knew he would not be offended, at least not for long, by the fact that some of the others had laughed at him, and was glad when, a moment later, he smiled and told them, 'I suppose it's difficult to believe something like that exists when you haven't seen it. But then the Edge of the World exists and you haven't seen that. Which reminds me. I must ask Whiskers to tell me more about it.'

Leaving the others to think about what he had said, Black Tip got up and trotted down to the stream. Vickey was going to follow, but changed her mind. Better, she thought, that she stay, in case she might have to speak up for him.

Not having seen any of the strange creatures Old Sage Brush had spoken of, the badgers didn't know what to make of Black Tip's story. What did interest them was the old fox's reference to the giant ginger cats. Back at the sheep farm they had overheard the vixens talking among themselves. From what had been said, they knew the vixens were afraid of cats, and they wondered why.

It was Sniff who ventured to raise the matter, and even though she did so in a manner that indicated she didn't want to pry, Sinnéad, to her surprise, got up and without a word walked away. Vickey, if the truth be known, didn't really want to talk about it either. At the same time she knew Sniff was still recovering from the horrible experience with the farmer and his pig waste, and thought it might do her good to hear of other creatures' problems.

'It was on our other great journey,' she told the badgers. 'We lost our way, and as Old Sage Brush was saying, we strayed into man's place. We saw many strange and wonderful things, like the giant ginger cats. Man had them cooped up like chickens, so they couldn't harm us. Anyway, my cubs were growing within me. I wanted to get home.'

Vickey sighed, and She-la took up the story. 'She didn't know what she was doing. There were a lot of dangers on the way back, but it didn't seem to matter to her. All she wanted was to get home.'

'And what happened?' asked Sniff.

'A large cat and a small dog,' said She-la. 'They cornered her, and they'd have killed her, but for Black Tip.'

'What about Sinnéad?' asked Snout. 'What happened to her?'

'That was later,' said Vickey, 'when we were back in the Land of Sinna.' Somehow Vickey felt batter able to talk about Sinnéad's experience than her own. 'Our cubs had just been born. She was in an earth not far from where we were. Skulking Dog had gone out to hunt.' She sighed deeply again. 'There were some cats up in the evergreens. They had gone wild.'

'Their leader was a long-haired tom,' said She-la. 'Black and grey, almost as big as ourselves. They were giving us a lot of trouble, especially Hop-along.'

'One night,' Vickey recalled, 'when Skulking Dog had left to hunt, they went to his earth. Sinnéad was on her own with her cubs. She had four. I suppose she panicked. She just grabbed one cub and ran.'

'That was Twinkle,' said She-la. 'The one with the white mark on her forehead, like herself. You saw her back at Beech Paw.'

'When Skulking Dog returned,' Vickey continued, 'the other three cubs had gone. The cats had taken them. A little dog and two vixens.'

'I'm sorry,' said Sniff.

'She still can't bring herself to talk about it,' She-la added. 'I suppose it's hard to blame her.'

The badgers nodded, and Snout said, 'Well, at least there are no cats on the mountain, whatever else there might be.'

Having rested in the birch grove for a day and a night, they decided to move on. They could see the snow had gone from the mountain tops now, and some were shrouded in soft misty clouds. Drops of rain glistened on the heather and rushes trembled in the wind as they made their way across the lower slopes. The sheep that grazed like white dots among the withered ferns, would lamb later than those in the valley, and so posed no problem. Here and there they came upon other clumps of trees and bushes, and a brief halt was called whenever it appeared that Old Sage Brush or Hop-along might need rest.

Some parts of the mountainside were covered with new plantations, and during a stop at one of these they found to their surprise, that the boundary fence had been broken, and something had been feeding on the young evergreens. Here and there bark had been ripped from the trunks, while some of the branches had been stripped of their needles. No scent remained, even on the droppings that were scattered around the area, and the old fox reckoned it was the work of sheep, or, more likely, mountain goats.

Not wishing to alarm him, the others looked and listened, but kept their thoughts to themselves. They could see that the droppings were big, bigger than they might have expected from sheep or goats. They could also see that whatever had been responsible, had also been chewing the tops of the young trees, and it was obvious that even a mountain goat standing on its hind legs couldn't reach up that far. As a result, some of them now began to wonder, and not without a certain apprehension, if perhaps there might be some truth in Black Tip's story after all.

Leaving the plantations behind them, they continued down across the mountain. By this time they had split up into three groups. Black Tip, Vickey and Skulking Dog had gone ahead. The three younger foxes, who were engaging in various games as they went along, had fallen some distance behind. With them were the badgers who had found that the slower pace of the young foxes was fast enough for them. And between them, but much further down, were the others. Whiskers was leading this group, Sinnéad was lending her support to Old Sage Brush, and She-la was with her mate, Hop-along.

Everything went well until there was a flutter of wings and a covey of grouse rose in front of Whiskers. Hugging the ground with whirring wings, the birds soared over the heather and dropped out of sight a short distance away. Their presence had come as a surprise, even to the foxes, as the wind was behind them. Knowing that they would have landed not far away, Whiskers fell back to wait with Old Sage Brush and Hop-along, while Sinnéad and She-la crept forward. In spite of the wind, they all got a strong smell of grouse now, indicating that there were others in the heather, and when a few more took to the air, they realised that they had come upon, not just a covey, but a large concentration of birds.

Sinnéad and She-la also dropped to the ground and waited. They knew that the others higher up would either see or hear the grouse and join them in the hunt. What they didn't know was that they weren't the only hunters on the mountain.

It was the keen hearing of Old Sage Brush that first picked up the sound of voices and he warned the other members of his group that man was approaching. Just as the wind had blown the scent of the grouse away from them, so too it had plucked the voices of man from the mountain, and soon they realised he was quite close.

'I hear many voices,' said the old fox. 'Are they shooters?'

Whiskers was sitting upright so that he could get a clear view across the heather. 'They're carrying something.'

'Are they searching?'

'No,' said Hop-along. 'they're coming in a straight line.'

'Any dogs?'

'I can't seen any,' continued Hop-along. 'It's hard to tell with the heather.'

'If they keep going, they'll pass behind us,' said Whiskers. 'Do you think we should make a run for it?'

'If we run,' said the old fox, 'the grouse will betray our presence. If we sit tight, man may not notice us.'

'But what if there *are* dogs?' asked Hop-along.

Old Sage Brush eased himself down again. 'If the wind has blown man's voice across the mountain so that it did not come to our ears, perhaps it will blow our scent away from his dogs.'

A few moments later, Sinnéad and She-la hurried back to inform them that they had spotted shooters and dogs up ahead of them.

'Are they coming this way?' asked Hop-along anxiously.

She-la shook her head. 'They're waiting in small groups and their dogs are on a leash.'

Hop-along squeezed himself further down under the heather and took a deep breath. 'Thank goodness for that.'

'But what if those dogs get our scent?' asked Whiskers.

'The only scent they will get is from the grouse,' Old Sage Brush assured him. 'No. If they are sitting tight, so will we. As soon as man passes behind us, we should be able to slip away.'

The flight of the grouse had attracted the attention of the other foxes, and from their vantage points higher up they watched with growing concern at what was happening. What Old Sage Brush and his group couldn't know was that the shooters and dogs were in a series of positions that formed a huge semi-circle ahead of them, while another line of men were spreading out in a semi-circle behind them. Gradually the circle closed, leaving no way out. Old Sage Brush and Sinnéad, Hop-along and She-la, and the otter who was taking them to the Edge of the World, had walked into a trap.

FOURTEEN

The Horns of a Dilemma

Unknown to the creatures that journeyed across the mountain, they had strayed into an area where an enterprising estate owner had restocked his land with red grouse. This man knew from his experience with those who came to hunt deer that people from other countries were prepared to pay big money for a day's shooting, particularly when they could be assured of getting something special in return. Consequently, he had set about recreating the great grouse days of long ago.

In those days, it wasn't unusual for estate owners and their guests to bag hundreds of grouse in one day in what were known as driven shoots. Over the years the grouse had become scarce, even dying out in places, and various efforts had been made to reintroduce them. Now they were back on this mountain at least, sharing the heather with the red deer, and a new type of sportsman would pay for the privilege of thinning them out.

The season for grouse shooting was now well past, but the estate owner had obtained special permission for a driven shoot to demonstrate to the authorities that the project was worthy of official support. Seeing the line of men about to start driving the grouse towards them, the men with the guns watched and waited. The dogs that were on their leashes nearby, watched them, and the eye of officialdom watched them all. None of them saw the other creatures that were watching them, those that were caught in the middle.

The idea was that the line of men, wielding sticks, would beat the heather and drive the grouse forward across the guns. The dead birds would be picked up later, and the retrievers would make sure none of them was missed, so that each of the visitors would be able to boast of as big a bag as possible.

Further up the mountain, the other foxes were almost frantic as they realised that Old Sage Brush and his group were trapped. They knew it would be only a short time before the line of men came upon them, and that would be the end.

For their part, the three younger foxes looked around, wondering what they could do. Further across the mountain they could see Black Tip and the others and knew they were wondering the same thin. Realising that something was wrong, but unable to see what it was, the two badgers came galloping up. The young foxes ran to meet them and gathered around to tell them what was happening. As they did so, they became aware that while they had been following events below, something else had been observing them. There, standing on a ridge above them, surveying it all, was the creature Black Tip had told them about. It was a massive creature, or so it seemed from where they stood. Its horns were enormous. They were, as Black Tip had said, shaped like the branches of a tree and had many points.

Its shaggy mane conveyed an unmistakable impression of strength, and its fine sinewy legs suggested a good turn of speed. For all that it had, as Black Tip had said, the body of a cow and the tail of a rabbit.

'Now we're trapped too,' whispered Scab. 'If it charges we're done for.'

'Not if we split up,' said Stumpy. 'It can't chase all of us at the same time.'

'Maybe if we ran down towards the others,' suggested Needle Nine, 'it might run after us and frighten man away.'

'That's a very good idea,' said Stumpy, and turning to the badgers asked them, 'What do you think? Are you with us?'

'We're with you,' replied Snout. 'If we cant' stay ahead of it perhaps we can avoid it, but you keep going.'

They agreed, and immediately bounded down through the heather. Glancing back over their shoulders, they expected to see the great creature charging after them, only to find, to their surprise, that it hadn't moved. Skidding to a halt, they looked up at it, wondering what to do.

Scab was out of breath, more from excitement and fear than anything else. 'Perhaps,' he panted, 'it has already hunted for its food.'

'So what do we have to do to get it to follow us?' wondered Needle Nine.

The badgers were now eyeing the creature with their small glassing eyes. All they could see was an outline of it against the sky.

If it won't chase us, maybe we can chase it,' ventured Sniff.

'Chase it?' Scab was incredulous.

'And what if it turns on us with those huge horns?' asked Needle Nine.

'We spend our nights feeding among animals with horns,' Snout told them. 'Most times they just lie and watch us, Sometimes, especially during the day, they might get frisky and lower their horns at us, but I never heard of a badger been killed by one of them yet.'

'Or a fox,' added Sniff.

'But these horns are very big,' Stumpy told them, and fearing that they might not have been able to see them, stressed, 'They're like branches of trees, just as Black Tip said. And there are a lot of sharp points on them.'

'Don't worry,' said Sniff. '*We've* enough fat to protect us. We'll make it move. You just make sure it runs in the right direction.'

The great horned creature still hadn't moved, nor had the men who where now standing in a line behind Old Sage Brush and the others. The three young foxes spread out and from hiding places beneath the heather, watched as the two badgers split up and circled around to get behind the ridge where the creature was standing. Suddenly the creature turned its creamy rump to them and they knew the badgers were approaching it from the other direction.

A few moments later, Snout appeared on the ridge. Showing great courage, he advanced slowly to confront the creature.

Immediately it lowered its enormous horns and charged. With surprising agility, he backed out of range, and came around so that it followed and was once again facing down the mountain. The foxes were wondering where Sniff had got to when they saw her shuffling up behind. Snout, meanwhile, was holding his ground, and when the creature charged again, its lowered horns scythed through the heather, throwing clumps into the air. Seizing her chance, Sniff darted in behind it and nipped one of its hind legs.

With a roar of pain that struck fear in the hearts of the young foxes, and alerted the men below, the creature bounded down off the ridge, and swerving crazily among the heather, sped away down the mountain. In the hope that they could steer it in the direction of the men and perhaps frighten them away, the three foxes followed.

Across the mountain, Black Tip, Vickey and Skulking Dog had seen the badgers tackling the great horned creature on the ridge, but didn't quite know what was going on. They were more concerned with the dogs. Perhaps, they thought, if they could somehow attract the attention of the dogs, Old Sage Brush and his group could escape. The problem was that if they showed themselves, the dogs might be unleashed on them.

There was no horned monster on their part of the mountain, only the occasional wren that flitted ahead of them, and nothing was afraid of the wren, except perhaps the spiders it hunted in the heather. However, as the young foxes had recently discovered, a wren has a very strong sent, a scent out of all proportion to its size. This, of course, was well known to the older foxes, and it was Skulking Dog who came up with the idea of using the wren to attract the attention of the dogs.

So it was that as the line of beaters watched the stag careering down the mountainside towards them and their grouse, some of the dogs that were straining impatiently on their leashes beside the guns became aware of another bird in the heather nearby, a bird much smaller than a grouse but with a scent that was strong and tempting.

Knowing that if the stag ran between them and the guns, it would ruin the shoot, the beaters were frantically waving their arms and sticks in an effort to ward it off. Seeing them, it did swerve, but came across Needle Nine in the heather, and being acutely aware of the severe pain another of these small creatures had inflicted on one of its hind legs, it resumed its downward course flushing out a few grouse on the way.

Over at the gun positions, the dogs that had become excited by the wren were further confused now by the scent of fox. They began to bark and wriggle to get free, unsettling the dogs at the other positions. As their masters wrestled to calm them, some of the guns began to fire, only to find that the few grouse that crossed their sights were out of range. The beaters, who had turned to face the stag, were shouting at them to hold their fire. For some reason the beaters couldn't understand, the stag kept coming, and before they knew what was happening it was among them, swerving in panic and sending coveys of grouse in all directions. Other guns began to blaze now, and to add to the confusion, an otter and four foxes bolted from the heather. If the grouse were out of range of the guns, so also were the otter and foxes, and there was nothing the beaters could do to stop them escaping.

Later, when they had all come together again, the young foxes couldn't wait to tell of the great horned creature they had met on the mountain, and how they had put it to flight.

Vickey smiled and nodded. 'We saw it. I thought you were all very brave to do what you did.'

'Well, it wasn't really us,' admitted Scab. 'It was Snout and Sniff.'

'It took great courage to face such a horned monster,' Black Tip told Snout.

'Even to come face to face with it from behind,' said Needle Nine. He laughed. 'Well, you know what I mean.'

The others knew well what he meant, but the badgers dismissed what they had done with a degree of modesty the foxes had come to expect of them.

'Maybe if we had been able to see it better, we might have been more afraid,' said Snout. 'Isn't that right Sniff?'

His mate nodded. 'All I could see was its hind legs, and I doubt if it saw me.'

'And what about you?' Scab asked Black Tip. 'Did you see any monster on your side of the mountain.'

Black Tip smiled. 'Of course we did. And you wouldn't believe the size of it. It could touch the sky without even trying, and eat from the heather without even bending. The very smell of it filled the dogs with fear and they couldn't wait to get away. But surely you must have seen it.'

Vickey and Skulking Dog were smiling now too, as if it was a joke. The young foxes, of course, had seen no such thing, but having laughed at Black Tip's monster before, they weren't about to make the same mistake again. And so, while they had their doubts, they kept them to themselves.

At the foot of the mountains a wooded glen dipped before them, grey and indistinct in the driving rain. On either side, patches of evergreens seethed in a turbulence that failed to trouble the leafless oak and birch. Unlike the rowan, the occasional holly tree was still red with berries, and at a time when food was scarce, would see some of the birds through to the spring.

As if to remind the foxes that they were still in sheep country, a grey crow rose from the heathered slopes and wheeled away into the wind, while a sodden length of wool clung grimly to a strand of barbed wire.

For fox and badger alike, it was time to seek shelter. For the otter, it was the opposite. Rain was something to enjoy, something to indulge in. Furthermore, a valley meant a river, and a river meant fish.

Leaving the others in the undergrowth of a sloping birch wood, Whiskers set off in search of a pool that he had frequented on previous journeys to the Edge of the World. Where he joined the river, a stream of brown peaty water cascaded down the mountainside, gushing over the rocks and beneath overhanging banks in a bubbling, frothing headlong race to find a wider, more even path somewhere below.

Immersing himself in the fast-flowing water, he allowed himself to be carried along with it, sliding over rocks and slithering between them, then speeding through pools and searching the banks for whatever scents or sustenance he could find. Above him the rain swished through the bare oak and birch, soaking the bright green moss that it nurtured on their lower trunks and on the granite boulders beneath. Here and there it also swelled a multitude of other streams and rivulets, so that they too gushed down from the hillside to join him in one glorious headlong rush through the woods.

Merging with other, more substantial streams, the river gradually became wider. It bubbled over a stony bed at a more leisurely pace, and wound its way along the floor of the glen until it found a depth more suited to its size and that of the otter who swam with it. This was where Whiskers knew his pool to be, a pool where fish were to be found not far from the surface, and large yellow eels in the muddy bottom.

Streaking through the darkness of its depths, he searched it with an expertise no other could match, and having failed to find a single fish, trawled the mud from which he had pulled many an eel. Not an eel was to be found, and bounding up on to the bank, he shook himself vigorously and wondered what had gone wrong.

It was the strong-smelling droppings of another hunter that told him why he had drawn a blank. Hurrying over to investigate, he confirmed that they were the droppings of a mink. They were slimy and, as far as he was concerned, had a bad smell, not at all like those of his own kind which were usually fishy and, to his nose at least, quite nice.

A quick check of the area disclosed many similar droppings, suggesting that a colony of these smaller rivals had invaded the area. He also noted that they had been eating a variety of food, including sticklebacks, waterhen, rabbit, and even chicken.

Feeling rather disconcerted, he turned and made his way back to the top of the glen where his friends were still sheltering from the rain.

'Well?' asked Old Sage Brush. 'Is this the one?'

'This is the one,' Whiskers told him. He paused. 'But there's just one problem.'

'What's that?' asked Vickey.

'Part of the river has been invaded by mink.'

So what?' said Skulking Dog. 'All we have to do is go around it.'

Whiskers nodded. 'I know. But it's just . . . It's just that this river is the path I travel. It gives me guidance, and it gives me food. I don't see why I should hand over any of it to anything else.'

'But you won't be staying on the river,' said Sinnéad. 'You're only passing by.'

'I know,' said Whiskers, 'and I hope to pass this way again but the mink have taken it over. The pool where I always stop to fish is empty, and now their markers are on the bank which has been marked as otter territory for many generations.'

'There must be other pools,' said Hop-along, 'and other food besides fish.'

'Fish *is* my food,' the otter replied, 'but you must also watch out, for the mink will eat anything, even your food, and they have. They've been hunting rabbits and chickens.'

Black Tip nodded. 'That means man will be on the alert, maybe even putting out choking hedge-traps.' He looked at Hop-along, who had lost a paw in one of man's traps, and added, 'We must be careful.'

'What do you think we should do?' asked She-la.

'I was thinking maybe you might help me drive them out,' said Whiskers.

'Yes, that's what we could do, drive them out,' exclaimed Scab.

Needle Nine and Stumpy were on their feet now too, full of the same enthusiasm for the idea, but the old fox told them to calm down. As they settled back, somewhat reluctantly, he went on. 'Mink are creatures of the water, and we are not. If we were to go into the water after them, we would be as powerless as fish that are out of it. And if we were to go after them on land, we would risk running into the traps that may have been set for them.

The young foxes lowered their heads and said nothing. This was something they hadn't thought of.

'What do you think I should do then?' asked Whiskers.

The old fox raised his greying head towards the sky as he often did when he was thinking. 'The river is your hunting ground, and you know it better than any other.

The mink and the otter are also very much alike, maybe even members of the same family, so you must know the mink better than most. Perhaps . . . ' He thought for a moment, as if anxious to advise him, yet not wishing to offend him. 'Perhaps if you were to hunt like and otter, and think like a fox, you might find a way to evict them from your pool . . . '

Black Tip accompanied Whiskers to the edge of the wood, and there they paused for a moment to talk. The only sounds were those of the falling rain and a stream that tumbled down the side of the glen.

'What he's really saying,' said Black Tip, 'is that there's always a way, if you think about it. I wish I had a rabbit for every time he told us the same thing.'

Whiskers smiled. 'If I had been able to think like a fox, I wouldn't have got myself into trouble at the fish farm.'

Black Tip smiled now too, and added, 'If I had been able to swim like an otter, I could have been more help to you.'

FIFTEEN

Thinking Like a Fox

Not knowing quite what to do, Whiskers followed the stream down to the river. Moving with less enthusiasm this time, he made his way to the pool where on previous occasions he had sported with trout and feasted on eels before setting out on the last stage of his journey to the Edge of the World.

He was still bemoaning the fact that the mink had totally ignored the territorial markers which he and other otters had left there, when he heard the faint cry of an animal in distress. Thinking it might be another otter, perhaps even a female, he cautiously made his way forward until he was standing on a bare earthen ridge overlooking a small clearing. He was still wondering where the call had come from when he heard it again. It was louder this time, nearer. Making his way among the withered oak leaves that littered the floor of the clearing, he saw that man had made a number of holes in the soft soil and sunk lengths of plastic piping into them. Pieces of decaying fish and chicken lay at he bottom of some of the pipes, and in one he found something else, not one of his own kind, but a female mink.

Not feeling the least sympathetic towards the mink, but concerned that any creature should find itself in such a predicament, Whiskers inquired, 'What are you doing down there?'

'I came in for the food,' croaked the mink. 'But now I can't get out. I think man must have made these holes to trap us.'

Whiskers glanced around, and seeing no other mink asked, 'Where are your own kind? Why didn't they help you?'

'They wanted to help me, but they couldn't think of a way of getting me out. It was only with great reluctance that they moved on. You see, I'm the one they call the Mother Mink.'

'The Mother Mink?'

She nodded. 'Most of my followers are females, but I'm the oldest, and so they call me the Mother Mink. But please, can you help me to get out?'

'Why should I help you?' asked Whiskers. 'Why should I help any of you? You have left your mark where we had ours, and claimed the river where we have fished for generations. Not content with fish, you have also hunted near the homes of man and now you have drawn his wrath upon us. Why don't you go back where you came from and leave us alone?'

'All you say is true,' replied the mink. 'But where are we to go? To the cages where man kept us for our fur? The cages were we lived and died, eating only what man gave us, living only as long as he allowed us?' she shook her head. 'I think not. It took us many generations and much hardship to escape from that bondage, and now that we are free, are we not to live like other creatures?'

'Well, when you put it like that,' said Whiskers. 'But you and your kind have stripped these pools to the bone. There's nothing left for me.'

'I know food is scarce,' the mink told him. 'That is why I found myself down here. As the Mother Mink, I had to try it first. At least when we found it was a trap the others were safe. But . . . ', she faltered for a moment. 'If I don't get out, I will die of hunger, or at the hands of man – unless you help me.'

When he hesitated, she continued, 'There is one pool where there are some fish left. If you do help me, I will show you where it is.'

'If you know of this pool,' said Whiskers suspiciously, 'surely the others will know of it too, and will have taken the fish.'

She shook her head. 'No, the Mother Mink has some privileges, and that is one of them.'

Having already made up his mind to help the mink, Whiskers was thinking of what the foxes had told him back at the lake. If they could pull small fish from the river, perhaps he could pull a mink from a hole. 'All right,' he said, and swinging his tail over the edge, told her, 'See if you can catch that.'

By standing on her hind legs, the Mother Mink was just able to catch the tip of the otter's tail. Being much smaller and lighter than he was, her weight was no problem, and he quickly pulled her out.

It was only then that Whiskers realised other mink had come into the clearing. Reluctant to leave their mother figure, they had lingered on, and now surrounded the otter which they thought had come to attack her, their eyes and teeth flashing viciously as they prepared to drive him off.

'No, no,' the Mother Mink told them, 'the otter has not sought to harm me. On the contrary, he has delivered me from my living death, and now he will share my pool.'

Almost as suddenly as they had appeared, they were gone, and the Mother Mink led Whiskers to a spot on the river where, she assured him, fish were to be found. He immediately slipped into the water and scoured the pool for trout or eels, only to find that it contained nothing more than a shoal of sticklebacks. Returning to the bank, he shook the water from his fur, and protested, 'I thought you said it contained fish.'

'And so it does,' replied the Mother Mink.

'But you didn't tell me they were only small fish.'

The Mother Mink smiled. 'You didn't ask me. And if I had told you, would you have helped me out? Anyway, when fish are scarce, sticklebacks are better than nothing.'

Whiskers now began to suspect that mink were more intelligent than he had supposed. There was, he knew, a lot of truth in what the Mother Mink had said. At the same time he couldn't help thinking she had used him because he had a longer tail, and tricked him because all she had to offer by way of reward were a few sticklebacks.

The words of Old Sage Brush were now going through his mind, and the conversation he had had with Black Tip at the edge of the birch wood about what had happened back at the fish farm. 'I know a lake where there are plenty of fish,' he said. 'Big fish.'

The Mother Mink was immediately suspicious. 'Why are you telling me? If you know of such a place, why do you not keep it to yourself?'

'I have sampled these fish for myself,' he told her, 'but I was only passing through, on my way to . . . to somewhere else. If you like, I will show you where it is.'

The Mother Mink hesitated. She wasn't quite sure of the otter's motives in telling her this. However, food was scarce, so she said, 'All right. But the others must come with me.'

Whiskers nodded. 'Very well. When dusk comes I'll return and take you there.'

Hurrying back to the birch wood, Whiskers told the foxes and the badgers that he had come up with a plan to get rid of the mink. He didn't tell them all that had happened, in case they might think he had been fooled, but he told them he would be away for some time and that they should wait for him.

'In the morning,' he said, 'if the rain has stopped, you will see the sharp peak of a mountain beyond the valley. Follow it until it disappears from view behind the hills. You will then be at a bend on the river. Wait for me there in the woods. When I return we will continue our journey to the Edge of the World.'

'Is the Edge of the World much farther?' asked Hop-along.

Whiskers shook his head. 'Just beyond that peak.'

When darkness came, Whiskers collected the mink and set off at a brisk pace up the mountain. Without the old fox or Hop-along to slow him down, he galloped on, travelling non-stop night and day until he arrived back at the small lake where man was rearing the fish.

Following him up on to one of the rafts, the mink were immediately excited by the splashing of the fish, and ran around, necks outstretched, to see how they could get at them.

'You didn't tell me they were in a net,' said the Mother Mink.

Whiskers smiled. 'You didn't ask me. And if I had told you, would you have agreed to come? Anyway, I have sampled them, and so can you.'

'But how?' asked the Mother Mink. 'They are protected by the net.'

'There is always a way,' said Whiskers, 'if you think about it.' He turned to go. 'Maybe if you swim like a mink and think like an otter, you will find it.'

When the dawn came, the rain had gone and for the first time the foxes got a clear view of the wooded glen that lay before them. Here and there, farmsteads nestled among the trees and where there were no trees, sheep grazed in the fields. With their limited vision, the badgers couldn't see very much of this. Like the foxes they could hear the streams that tumbled from the mountain, and the deeper sound of the river somewhere below, but even the foxes couldn't see the river. The reddish brown twigs of birch trees formed a canopy that hid it from the eyes of all but those who had cause to go down to the very bottom.

Beyond the valley was a low hill partly covered by evergreens, and beyond that the sharp peak of a mountain. The peak was blue and pointed into clouds that were as white and fluffy as lambs' wool. Acting on the otter's instructions, foxes and badgers set off in the direction of the peak, and knowing that man had put out traps for the mink, they kept well above the farmsteads. In places, rocks that had once streamed down the side of the valley littered their path, and these helped conceal their passage from one patch of evergreens to another.

As the morning wore on, a wintry sun betrayed the silvery strands of spiders' webs that spanned the clumps f heather, and glinted on the river when it emerged from the trees to wind between bare rocky slopes. At one stage, Skulking Dog told Black Tip he had come across a tuft of badger hair, but in view of what had happened the last time Snout and Sniff had visited some of their own kind, they decided not to say anything about it.

The sharp peak, which was streaked as if with snow, gradually grew larger until it was almost looming over them, and then, just as Whiskers had predicted, it began to disappear behind a horizon of green fields. At the same time, the river began to sweep around through heavily wooded banks, and they knew this was where they were to wait for him.

'You know something,' whispered Scab when some of the older foxes and the badgers were sleeping.

'What?' asked Stumpy.

'I'm beginning to think there's no such thing.'

Needle Nine was searching for a black spider he had seen escaping from a small puff ball he had just stood on. 'No such thing as what?' he asked absent-mindedly.

'As the Edge of the World. I mean, we've been travelling for a long time, and there's no sign that we're getting any nearer to it.'

The black spider had disappeared over a lichen-covered rock and Needle Nine abandoned the search for it. 'You know, I'm beginning to have my doubts too,' he confided. 'I keep expecting to see it around the next bend in the river, but all we ever see is more river, and more bends.'

'But why would they want to bring us on such a journey if there's no end to it?' asked Stumpy.

Scab shook his head. 'They said it was to get away from the sheep, but there were plenty of places we could have stayed until the lambing was over. Places with all the food we needed, and no choking hedge-traps.'

'That's true,' said Stumpy, 'but you heard Old Sage Brush yourself. He has this idea in his head that he wants to go to the Edge of the World, and nothing will stop him. I just hope Whiskers isn't having him on.'

'Well, if we don't reach it soon,' declared Scab, 'I'm going to look for my own territory.'

'Me too,' said Needle Nine.

Stumpy nodded and admitted, 'I know what you mean. The way I feel at the moment I'd rather see a young vixen than the Edge of the World.'

The vixens, who were lying nearby, opened their eyes and looked at each other. They said nothing, but each of them knew what the other was thinking. If Whiskers didn't return soon, the young foxes would look elsewhere for the land of their dreams.

Fortunately, Old Sage Brush had not heard the young foxes. He did not doubt for a moment that Whiskers would return, or that he would lead them to the Edge of the World, just as he had promised to do.

When eventually the otter did return, it was obvious that he had travelled a long distance and needed to rest. Faced with yet another delay, the young foxes could no longer hide their impatience and openly expressed the doubts they had about ever reaching the end of their journey. Embarrassed that one of hers should have so little faith, She-la rebuked them, saying they should have more patience, but the old fox told her there was no need. 'When we are young and fast, like they are,' he said, 'time moves slowly. And when we are old and slow, like I am, time moves fast.' Then, addressing the younger foxes, he added, 'But who is in such a hurry that he does not want to hear how the otter lured the mink away from his pool? And who would deny him time to hunt in a river that is now being joined by other rivers on the final part of its journey?'

Realising that they had talked when they should have listened, and doubted when they should have known better, the young foxes cocked their ears. Their sensitive hearing picked up the gurgling of another river and they knew that what the old fox had said was true.

Later, when Whiskers had rested, She-la told him, more by way of apology than explanation, 'They think they'll never see the Edge of the World.'

Whiskers smiled, and turning to the young foxes, said, 'I know exactly how you feel. Sometimes I feel the same myself. But we haven't far to go now.' He wiped his whiskers with a forepaw, and added, 'But you know, you won't find all your dreams at the end of the bow.'

The young foxes eased themselves down and waited to hear what he had to say.

'On my journeys to the Edge of the World,' he continued, 'I dream of many delights I know I will encounter along the way.' Seeing that he had a captive audience now, he rolled over on his back and looking up at the sky, told them, 'Even though I have travelled the same way before, each journey is a new experience. I find new streams, I chase new fish, I sniff new scents, and if I'm lucky, I make new friends. Sometimes I think I cannot wait until I find my pool, for when it is full of fish, it is one of my greatest delights, an exquisite delight, a delight that I could not possibly share with the mink. Then I cannot wait until I find something else, something quite different, something so, so utterly enjoyable that it is quite . . . quiet indescribable.'

Needle Nine squirmed forward, his eyes wide with wonder at what Whiskers was saying. 'What?' he asked. 'What's so indescribable.'

Whiskers shook his head. 'I . . . I can't describe it.' He paused, and the older foxes smiled. 'Even if I could describe it, you wouldn't believe it unless you saw it for yourself.'

'You mean, you'd show us?' asked Scab.

Rolling back on to all fours, Whiskers nodded. 'If we had time but then, I know you're anxious to be on your way.'

'We're not in that much of a hurry,' said Stumpy. 'But what is it?'

'Well, it's not the Edge of the World,' replied Whiskers, 'but it's not far from it.'

Old Sage Brush smiled. 'Otter, he said, 'we'll make a fox out of you yet. But if this thing you describe is so indescribable, how am I going to see it?'

'You will not need to see it,' Whiskers replied. 'It will be enough for you to hear it.'

The badgers had just awakened in time to hear what Whiskers had been saying.

'We too have our delights,' said Snout, and rolling over so that his shoulders were against the trunk of a young beech tree, added in syllables that coincided with each rub. 'The, exquisite, indescribable, pleasure of rubbing an itching back against a tree.' Then he began to scratch his enormous belly which he obviously felt was beginning to get slack. 'And then there are other delights that are equally indescribable, the delight of slurping on the most sumptuous, the most succulent, the most satisfying thing in the whole world.'

'What's that?' asked Whiskers, who was beginning to think that perhaps he had missed out on something.

'A worm!' declared Snout, and with a squeal of laugher he bounced off through the trees with Sniff to gorge themselves, as they did every night, on a diet of worms, beetles and anything else they could extract from the earth.

Whiskers smiled. 'As I was saying, there are other delights besides eating, and this one I think you will like to see.' He too galloped off through the trees, and curious to know what he was talking about, the foxes got up and took off after him.

Emerging from the woods, Whiskers led them up across the fields until he came to a road. For a moment they hung back as one of man's machines lumbered past. Then, when they had expelled the pungent fumes from their nostrils, they followed him up the side of a hill, the top of which was covered with evergreens. Beyond the evergreens, the sound of falling water came to their ears, and they found themselves on the rim of another valley.

Hearing the others take a sharp intake of breath, Old Sage Brush asked, 'What is it?'

'It's . . . it's like the Edge of the World,' said Vickey.

'It *is* the Edge of the World,' whispered Needle Nine.

Whiskers smiled. 'Not quite, but as I told you, it's not far from it.'

'The water seems to be falling a long way,' observed the old fox.

'It is,' said Vickey. 'It almost took my breath away. I wish you could see it. The side of the valley is very steep here, almost straight, and the river is falling down it in long silvery threads. Sometimes the wind catches it and blows it this way and that, but nothing stops it, not even the rocks. The noise you hear is it crashing down to the bottom where it becomes a river again.

'How far down does it go?' asked the old fox, who was trying to imagine it.

'Almost as far as the eye can see,' Black Tip told him.

'Even the trees on the bottom look small from up here,' added Sinnéad.

The light was beginning to fade now. 'Wait here,' said Whiskers, and racing back to a spot where the side of the valley didn't drop as sharply as it did at the waterfall, he began to make his way down.

'It's very steep,' said Scab. 'I hope he makes it.'

'How is he going to get back up?' wondered Stumpy.

By the time Whiskers had reached the lower slopes, he seemed to have become very small. Pausing only briefly to look up at them, he quickly made his way across to the foot of the waterfall. There they saw him play as never before, dashing in and out of the silvery spray, swimming through the foaming pools, scrambling up the rocks and slithering back in, in a non-stop cycle of sheer enjoyment. Not even the young foxes begrudged him his precious moments beneath the fall, and they settled down to watch and wait.

Man, who also enjoyed the beauty of this place, had gone and the only other creature to see the otter was a peregrine falcon that soared silently overhead.

Vickey rose quickly to her feet, then settled back down again.

'What's the matter?' asked She-la.

'It was one of those birds that took Young Black Tip shortly after he was born.'

'What happened?' asked stumpy.

'It dropped him in the lake. If it hadn't been for Whiskers he would have drowned.'

'At least you got yours back,' said Sinnéad.

Vickey was sorry she had mentioned the matter now, and was glad when, a few moments later, Whiskers seemed to decide he had soaked up enough of the waterfall. Darkness was closing in, and almost as if an even greater delight had suddenly beckoned him, he was away, running, swimming and floating down the river that wound its way across the bottom of the valley.

'Come on,' said Black Tip, 'he's on his way to the Edge of the World and I don't think he's going to stop until he gets there!'

SIXTEEN

Creepy Crawlies

Seeing Whiskers making a sudden dash down the river, the foxes raced back through the trees. At the edge of the evergreens, they stopped only long enough to make sure the way was clear, then hurried down the darkened hillside to the bend of the river. There they collected Snout and Sniff, and arrived at the spot where the two rivers joined in time to see Whiskers scrambling out. Without as much as a look in their direction, he shook the water from his coat, and galloped off through the trees. Foxes and badgers followed, and were relieved when, a short time later he slowed down to what they considered to be a safer pace.

The river was wider now, but still quite shallow, and it glinted in the light of the moon as it wound its way through the wooded banks of large estates where horses grazed and exotic pines swayed in the breeze. Here and there they crossed the river and took short-cuts across the bends. At one spot the moon lit up a great stone bird with hooked beak and staring eyes that guarded the entrance to an estate. It was a frightening figure and not knowing it was made of stone, they were happy to stay in the shadows and slip quietly past.

This was an area where various rivers and streams flowed through heavy vegetation, an area where a badger might dig or a fox might dally, but Whiskers was not to be delayed or deflected from his path. He kept going and eventually all the water courses became one to emerge as a wide, deep river that flowed as quietly as those that trotted along beside it.

Buildings began to loom up out of the darkness, and when they had passed beneath a bridge, something new began to assail the sensitive noses of both fox and badger. It was something quite different from the smell of the country, different even from the smell of man.

'What is it?' asked Sniff, who had stopped and with raised nose was trying to determine what it was.

'That' whispered Whiskers, 'is the smell that tells us we're almost there. It's the smell of the water at the Edge of the World!'

Turning their noses into the salt breeze once more, they continued along the path until they came to another bridge.

There, they found, the path ran out. So also, they sensed, did the river, but where it went to, they couldn't tell. They paused for a moment and the cry of strange birds came to their ears. Whiskers led them through gently lapping water and up around rocks until they were on the bridge. Beyond the bridge more buildings loomed up, and from inside a large dog barked. As with the great stone bird, they slipped quietly past, and then something else assailed their senses, not a smell this time, but a noise. It was a noise not unlike the waterfall, only much greater, and they knew without asking that it must be the sound of the river tumbling over the Edge of the World.

Whiskers took them to a cave in an earthen bank, and while he hunted they listened in a mixture of apprehension and wonder to the great noise that filled the world outside. Not knowing what lay before them, and fearful that they might fall over the edge, they all accepted that hunting was not for them that night. Nor it seemed, was sleep, until at last, just before dawn, exhaustion proved too much and despite their fears they drifted into a world in which they were looking over the edge of an abyss and long silvery threads of water were pouring down into a chasm of endless darkness.

The reality proved vastly different. When, some time later Whiskers arrived, those that could see awakened to find a great blue lake stretching away before them. Arching over the water was the Bow in the Cloud, sharper and more colourful than they had ever seen before. One end of the bow, they knew, was back in the Land of Sinna, and it was plain to see that the other end had nothing to rest on. It simply dropped over the edge.

It was a matter of great regret to all of them that Old Sage Brush couldn't see what he had travelled so far to find. In typical fashion, he himself expressed no regret, but listened carefully as first one, then another told him about all the wondrous things they could see. The noise, they explained, was caused by the water rolling in to the stony shore, the birds that cried in the wind, the same big white birds that followed man when he was turning the fields. Occasionally they saw strange objects moving slowly in the distance, and these, Whiskers explained, were the things man used to travel along the Edge of the World. Sometimes, he said, they disappeared over the edge, and occasionally, when storms stirred up the water, they were thrown about like a leaf in a stream.

'Sometimes,' he told them, 'the storm throws them up, just as an owl throws up the bits of food it does not want.'

'It seems to throw up many things,' observed Hop-along, indicating the pieces of wood, plastic floats, seaweed and other flotsam that had been washed up on the stony shore.

'There's no danger of me throwing up anything,' grumbled Skulking Dog. 'My stomach's empty.'

'There's some food under the weed and stones,' Whiskers told him. 'Here. Let me show you.' He galloped down to the shore and returning with a crab, cracked it open. It didn't provide much food, barely a mouthful in fact, but they could see that he relished it greatly. 'And there are other things under the weeds, creepy crawlies that some of you will just adore.'

Realising that he was referring to them, Snout and Sniff galloped down towards the water's edge, and immediately began poking their long noses in under stones and seaweed and anything else that might be hiding a tasty morsel.

Hearing them slurping and crunching everything they could find, Black Tip smiled. 'Give me a rabbit any time.'

'Or a chicken,' added Skulking Dog.

'You will find plenty of rabbits, among the sand dunes,' Whiskers assured them. 'But not now. Later, when darkness has come and man has gone.'

They could see it was the otter's custom to lie up in this cave during the day, and if they had any doubt about the wisdom of doing so, it was quickly dispelled when they heard barking nearby. The young foxes were on their feet in an instant, but Whiskers advised them to sit tight and be quiet.

Peering out, they could see the badgers had turned to face a small dog, although now that they looked at it, they weren't quite sure if it was a dog. It was white, but its coat had been cut in a way that made it bald in parts and fluffy in others.

'And that's not all,' Vickey told Old Sage Brush. 'It's wearing another coat, like the ones man wears.'

'I don't think it's going to attack,' said Hop-along, assuring himself more than anything else. 'It's just standing back barking.'

A few minutes later they heard a voice calling the dog, and after a few more barks, it turned and ran off.

The old fox chuckled. 'Well, if that doesn't beat all. A fancy haircut? And man's coat?'

Vickey nodded. 'It was strapped around it to keep it warm.'

'It's more than man does for us,' said She-la. 'But maybe as Whiskers says, he's different here.'

Scab smiled. 'I could do with a new coat. Maybe he'll give me one!'

Just then, the badgers came lumbering back. They were slightly out of breath from the excitement of their brief encounter, and while they felt the odd-looking dog had posed no real threat to them, they decided they too should wait until darkness before exploring this strange new world.

Neither man nor dog returned, and they all lay up in the cave, undisturbed for the rest of the day. Only when the moon came up and was sparkling on the soft undulating swell of the sea did they make a move. There were, as Whiskers had said, rabbits in the dunes and creepy crawlies on the shore. These the badgers and foxes hunted, each to their own liking, while the otter searched the depths that the others would never see, floating on his back to eat his catch and grinning back at the moon.

Occasionally Whiskers returned to the cave with crabs, or fish that were too large to eat at sea, and what was left over never went to waste. Even though Old Sage Brush didn't have all his teeth, he found a way of cracking crab shells, while Hop-along discovered that one paw could pin a wriggling fish just as well as two.

When the younger foxes weren't hunting rabbits in the sand dunes, they were down at the stony shore with the badgers, playing duels with the snapping claws of the crabs and seeking out the creepy crawlies that played hide and seek with the tide.

However, nature, like the tide, was now playing games with the young foxes, pulling them to the shore for cubbish fun, yet filling their minds with other more mature thoughts, and one morning, just before dawn, they decided to explore the fields behind the sand dunes to see if there were any other foxes in the area. As the vixens had observed, the urge to find a mate was coming upon them more strongly with each night that passed.

Leaving the shore to the badgers, the three of them made their way up through a crevice in the cliff. Beyond the sand dunes they found bare fields. These still bore the scent of man, so they continued along a fence until they came to rougher land that held out more promise.

The sound of the sea and the smell of the salt were still in the air, but now they detected other scents, including one that told them a strange vixen had been in the area earlier in the night. Following this scent they came to a high bank, the sides of which were covered in gorse, and there they found the strangest traces of all. Something had left long silvery streaks on the top, and as they sniffed to try to find out what it was the creature came slithering out of the darkness and was upon them in an instant.

Throwing themselves back down the bank, they tumbled on to the field in time to see a monstrous caterpillar sliding past, and even though it was still quite dark, they were so close that they could see right through its skin.

'Look what it's been eating!' exclaimed Stumpy.

Picking themselves up, they raced back to the cave and burst in upon the others with the news.

'We saw it! We saw it!' exclaimed Scab.

'Saw what?' asked Old Sage Brush.

'The caterpillar,' panted Needle Nine. 'The one Ratwiddle was talking about before we left the Land of Sinna.'

The others gathered around anxious to hear more.

'Is this true?' Vickey asked Stumpy.

Stumpy nodded. 'It had been hunting man, just as Ratwiddle said it would.'

'And it nearly gobbled us up too,' added Scab.

'It left long slimy tracks behind it,' said Needle Nine. 'Come on, we'll show you.'

Daylight was just beginning to break beyond the Edge of the World as the young foxes led their elders across the fields to the place where four silvery streaks emerged from the grey light of dawn and stretched away into the dimly-lit distance.

Old Sage Brush put his nose to one of them. It was smooth and had a scent that he didn't recognise.

They were all sniffing the silvery streaks now and professing their puzzlement, when Stumpy cried, 'Look, here it comes again!'

In their anxiety to get out of the way, the others pushed the old fox with them, and as they came to rest at the bottom of the embankment they looked up to see the caterpillar framed against the morning sky. It was green, just as Ratwiddle had predicted it would be, and as it slid quietly past them, Skulking Dog whispered, 'They're right. It has been feeding on man.'

'We could see right through its skin,' Vickey told the old fox.

Knowing how difficult it must be for Old Sage Brush to imagine such a thing, the others told him they too had seen man inside the caterpillar. He was, they explained, all wrapped up and staring ahead with unseeing eyes, tucked in here and there like a fly that had been wrapped in a spider's thread and put aside for eating later.

When the train disappeared into the distance, the foxes returned to the cave. There they pondered on what they had seen, but neither they, nor the badgers, nor indeed the otter, could explain it. In any event, they were safe in their cave for the time being, their bellies were full, and it was time to sleep.

Whatever about the older foxes, the dreams of the younger ones were filled with visions of caterpillars, great green caterpillars that slithered up out of the darkness and threatened to gobble them up ... For them it was a restless sleep, and when once again the caterpillar came upon them, they heard the scream of a young vixen coming across the fields beyond the silvery streaks. Or was it their own cries of alarm that had awakened them?

The others were awake now too, and they realised that the screaming that had wrenched them from their sleep was coming from above. Looking up, they saw several large gulls chasing another gull. The other bird had food in its mouth, and as they wheeled and dipped, and screamed again, it was forced to let it go. Slowly the food fell to the ground, and before the foxes knew what was happening, Whiskers had slipped out of the cave and was galloping down across the stones to claim it.

'Must be a crab,' observed Hop-along.

'He's too late,' said Sinnéad. 'Look. Another otter.'

So it was, but if they were expecting to see Whiskers fight for what the seagull had dropped, it was not to be.

The other otter was chickering now, head lowered as it laid claim to the food. Only when it had finished did Whiskers approach, and even then they did not fight. Instead they touched noses, and racing down to the water's edge, slipped into the sea. For a moment they could be seen swimming in complete unison, twisting and turning, rising and diving, enjoying the company of each other and the soft embrace of the sea. Then they were gone.

SEVENTEEN

Daisybright

It was no surprise to the older foxes, or indeed to the badgers, that Whiskers didn't return. They knew he had found what he had dreamed of, and while they were sorry to lose him, their hopes were now raised that they would realise their dreams too, and discover that friendlier hand which, he had assured them, was to be found here at the Edge of the World.

The reality of what had happened hadn't yet sunk in to the younger foxes, a fact that became evident when Old Sage Brush remarked rather wistfully. 'Well, that's the last we'll see of him.'

'How do you mean?' asked Needle Nine.

'He came for a mate didn't he? And now he's found her.'

Stumpy and Scab bounded down to the water's edge to see if they could get another glimpse of the otters, and Needle Nine raced after them.

'I think it's time we found some of our own kind too,' said Vickey.

The old fox nodded. 'When gloomglow comes, and the others are out hunting, perhaps we should find what lies on either side of us. I suggest you and Black Tip go one way. And Sinnéad, you and Skulking Dog go the other.'

'What about the caterpillar?' asked Sinnéad.

Knowing that they were all wondering about the caterpillar, the old fox said, 'Well, I've been thinking about that. We saw it twice. Or at least you saw it once and the young foxes saw it once. And it appears to me that each time it comes out it follows its own tracks. If that's so, then you've nothing to worry about. Just stay out of its way and leave it to man.'

The small birds that flocked around the tiny harbour at the mouth of the river had gone. Fast in flight and in their walk across the shingle, where they turned stones in search of food, they would return at daybreak. Only a cormorant lingered on, diving for long periods where the salt water mixed with the fresh. It was oblivious to the fading light and too intent on what it was doing to notice the two foxes recrossing the bridge.

Taking great care to avoid both man and dogs, Black Tip and Vickey kept to the shadows of walls that were built to hold back the sea and boats that would ride out the winter on stilts. While Whiskers had promised that man would be friendlier at the Edge of the World, man was still man and dogs were dogs, and this was proving to be a very peculiar place indeed.

Not far beyond the bridge, strange sounds brought Black Tip and Vickey to an abrupt halt. Venturing closer, they saw many lights flashing on and off, lights that were so brightly coloured they looked as if they had come from the Bow in the Cloud. Children laughed as very small horses and large wooden birds carried them around in circles, and that perhaps was the strangest thing of all, for although they watched for some time, they never once saw the hooves of the horses touching the ground.

Farther on they looked up in wonder at what they took to be a large spotted worm. Or was it an eel? They couldn't be sure. It was curled around a structure that was clearly of man's making so that its tail was in the air and its head was on the ground. Its eyes were large and staring, and it had a huge gaping mouth. For all that it took no notice of them, or of anything else that passed. What they would have thought if children had come sliding down out of its mouth, no one knows.

Leaving the merry-go-round and other seaside entertainments, Black Tip and Vickey went back to the cave. Skulking Dog and Sinnéad were already there, and when the four of them reported to the others what they had seen, they had no difficulty in deciding which way they should go. Members of their own kind, they knew, were more likely to be found in the shadows, so they turned their backs on the bright lights and continued along the Edge of the World.

While the foxes took care to keep away from the great green caterpillar, the badgers had no such inhibitions. If the truth be known, it was far too big for them to see, and what they couldn't see didn't frighten them. In any event, caterpillars were a welcome part of their diet, when they could find them, and where there were large caterpillars, they reckoned there were bound to be small ones! They found that the slime the creature left seemed to nurture gorse and briars and all the other kinds of cover in which they loved to browse. It also hurried past, as if it was afraid of badgers, and it came as no surprise to them when, one night, they came upon a sett on the bank beside the silvery streaks.

The fact was, they could see little of the shiny railway tracks, except where they glinted in the moonlight, but they noticed that sometimes the bank went up to them. Other times it went down to them, and it was in a place where it went down that they came across the sett. It was well hidden beneath the gorse and briars, and was obviously occupied.

The discovery filled Sniff with great joy, but then as she thought of what had happened to the badgers she had befriended back at the pig farm, she was filled with a sense of foreboding. Pausing at the entrance to the sett, she turned to Snout and asked, 'What if I bring trouble upon this family too?'

'You didn't bring trouble upon the others,' he assured her. 'It was man.'

Still, she hesitated, and as she did so, the snout of a boar badger emerged from the sett. Suspicious of the strangers, he immediately bared his teeth and stayed where he was to block the way.

'We mean you no harm,' Snout assured him. 'We've come a long way and are just trying to make contact with our own kind.'

'Where have you come from?' asked the other badger.

'From a land beyond the great peak.'

There was a scuffle and a shuffle, and the boar was pushed aside by his mate. 'Why did you leave?' she asked.

'Man destroyed our sett, our young, everything,' Sniff explained.

'You poor thing,' said the sow, and with a display of the greatest compassion, told them to come in.

'You'll find man much friendlier here,' said the boar, when they had settled in the warmth of the den.

The earth shook as the great green caterpillar slithered past once more.

'Our friends are afraid of the caterpillar,' said Sniff. 'They say it eats man.'

The other two badgers laughed, and the boar asked, 'Who told you that?'

'The foxes,' replied Snout. 'They travelled with us.'

'Well tell your fox friends the caterpillar will do them no harm, as long as they keep out of its way.'

'And does it really eat man?' asked Sniff.

The other sow smiled and shook her head. 'We've seen man inside it all right. But we've also seen him walk out again. We think it's something he uses to take him from one place to another.'

Realising this was something the country badgers couldn't comprehend, the sow changed the subject, saying, 'But you must be hungry. Come, we'll get you something to eat.'

Expecting to be shown a patch of soft earth where they could grub for worms, Sniff and Snout followed them across the fields until they came to a row of houses. Dogs barked, but the sow told them, 'Don't worry. They're in their own gardens. Where we're going there are no dogs.'

Where they were going was the back garden of a house whose sole occupant, an elderly lady, had encouraged badgers to feed from the dishes she left out each night. Unable to sleep, she passed her nights watching these creatures venture into the circle of light at the back of her house, and now as she eased aside the curtain, she smiled with the pleasure of seeing two strange badgers joining the two she already knew.

'So Whiskers was right,' said Old Sage Brush, when Snout and Sniff returned to tell them what they had found.

'And what about foxes?' inquired She-la.

'We didn't ask.' Sniff lowered her head. 'Sorry.'

'Not to worry,' said the old fox. 'But perhaps you won't mind if one of us goes back with you to find out . . . I take it you are going back to the sett, aren't you?'

Snout nodded. 'This is as far as we go. We've found what we came for.'

'I'm glad,' said the old fox. 'Take good care and keep an eye on that caterpillar.'

Sniff smiled. 'Don't worry. We will.'

When the badgers were saying their goodbyes to the others, Old Sage Brush called Stumpy and Scab to one side. 'I want you to go with them,' he said. 'If there's a badger sett on that bank, there just might be a fox earth.'

'And if there isn't?' asked Stumpy.

'Then I think you should have a look at that garden. No need to mention it to the badgers. That's something they'll want to keep to themselves. But it should be easy enough to back-track on their scent and find it.'

'What's the point of going to the garden?' asked Scab.

'Well, if you were a fox living in this area, and you knew someone was feeding badgers, what would you do?'

The two young foxes thought for a moment.

'Have a look?' suggested Stumpy.

'To see if there was anything left,' added Scab.

The old fox nodded. 'That's right. I'd be dropping in there occasionally, on the off chance that the badgers might have missed something.

Snout and Sniff were getting ready to go now.

'What about Needle Nine? asked Scab.

'He's out hunting with Skulking Dog at the moment. When he returns he can follow you.'

The badgers who lived on the railway bank had occasionally come across fox scents, but were not aware of any earths in the vicinity of their sett. Stumpy and Scab did a quick check of the area just to make sure, and after thanking the badgers, took their leave. However, instead of returning to the others, they picked up the strong scent the four badgers had left on their way to and from the garden, and followed it. They found the sounds and scents at the back of the houses strange, even frightening, especially the barking of dogs that started up behind the garden walls as soon as they approached. More than once they were tempted to turn tail and run, but they held their ground. They reckoned that if the dogs hadn't been able to attack the badgers, they wouldn't be able to attack them, and a short time later they were concealed in a tangle of undergrowth at the end of a wooded garden.

There was also a strong tangle of scents in the garden. Besides those of the badgers, there were the scents of small birds, magpies, cats, and of course, man. The bowls which had been left out for the badgers were still sitting in the light at the back door, and more than once as they waited, the young foxes wondered if there was any food left in them.

As it turned out, they weren't the only ones. A short time later, another young fox appeared from the shadows and tip-toed into the light. Pausing now and then to listen and look around, it cautiously approached one of the bowls.

'Wait there,' whispered Stumpy, and before Scab could object, he padded quietly across the lawn to where the other fox was now sniffing around the bowls.

'Did you find anything?' he asked.

Startled, the other fox turned around, and his heart gave an extra beat when he saw it was a vixen, 'Sorry, I didn't mean to frighten you. My name's Stumpy. What's yours?'

The young vixen's ears were erect, her eyes wide. 'Daisybright,' she blurted.

Scab was beside Stumpy now and they had a fleeting glimpse of another young vixen at the edge of the shadows. At the same time, they became aware of a cat in the vicinity, and before they could say anything more, the vixens were gone.

Taking off after them, they followed their scent as far as the silvery tracks of the great green caterpillar, and were considering what to do when Needle Nine caught up with them.

'You should have seen her,' exclaimed Stumpy. 'She was beautiful!'

'Who was?' asked Needle Nine

'She was in the garden. She had the most beautiful eyes you could ever imagine, and her name, it was lovely too. Daisybright . . . '

'The vixen that was with her was beautiful too,' said Scab, 'but I didn't get a chance to speak to her.'

'There wasn't' a third one by any chance?' asked Needle Nine, clearly disappointed that he had missed them.

The others shook their heads, and Scab said, 'They've gone across the caterpillar tracks.'

'Do you think we should follow?' asked Needle Nine. 'The badgers said the caterpillar won't harm us, as long as we keep out of its way.'

'All right,' said Stumpy. 'But we had better be careful.'

To their surprise, they found that the vixens hadn't crossed the tracks, but run alongside them. Following their scent, they came to what appeared to be the entrance to a huge earth, and were considering whether they should venture inside when the great caterpillar came charging out of it. Cowering back, they waited in fear and trembling until it had passed, then scurried back to the others.

For several nights following their encounter, the young foxes visited the garden again in the hope that Daisybright and her friend might return. They didn't, and seeing how deeply disappointed the young foxes were, Old Sage Brush suggested that they should all continue along the tracks of the caterpillar in the hope of making contact with them. This they did, hiding when the caterpillar came, and generally making sure to stay well out of its reach. Along the way they made contact with other foxes, but of Daisybright and her friend there was no sign. Eventually, with the help of one of the other foxes they met, they made their way to an old house, and under the floorboards, found a comfortable den.

There they settled in, hunting the gardens by night and watching the Edge of the World by day. The only competition was from cats that also hunted in the gardens, and while Vickey and Sinnéad had considerable difficulty in coming to terms with this, they had to accept that the cats had been there first, and that they must give way to them.

In between day-dreams of Daisybright and her friend, the young foxes also watched the trawlers come and go, floating as Whiskers would have said, like a leaf upon the water. Sometimes they would see man walking around on them and they knew that another of Ratwiddle's prophecies had come true.

Often the trawlers were followed by flocks of gulls, and as that signalled the presence of food, they got into the habit of going down to a little harbour in the early hours of the morning to see what they could get.

It was in this way that Stumpy met Daisybright again. She too had come down to the harbour to meet the trawlers, and this time she was more receptive to his approach. She told him she and her sister lived in the Field of the Standing Stones, and as soon as she succeeded in getting a fish, she headed back there. Seizing the opportunity, he trotted along beside her.

In addition to the standing stones, there were a number of small buildings in the field, and following Daisybright into an earth that had been dug at the base of one of these, Stumpy found himself in her den. It was, he discovered when his eyes became accustomed to the darkness, unlike any other earth he had ever been in. Man-made boxes were stacked on either side, and on top of one of these was a cat. Daisybright left the fish on the floor for the cat and when it hopped down, he could see it was deformed in as much as its hind legs were longer than its front ones. The deformity, however, was greatly to its advantage when it was jumping back up, and it returned to its perch with one easy leap.

It was the first time Stumpy had ever seen a fox sharing an earth with a cat, but then, he thought, he had seen other foxes sharing earths with badgers, even rabbits, so he just said, 'I've never seen an earth like this before.'

Daisybright smiled. 'But then you're from the country, aren't you?'

He nodded, and looking up at the boxes, asked, 'What's in those?'

'Man, of course.'

Startled, Stumpy took a step back.

Daisybright laughed. 'Don't worry. He's dead.'

'Dead?'

'That's right. This is where man comes when he dies.'

'How do you know?'

Daisybright smiled impishly. 'We've seen his bones?'

In the nights that followed, Scab also visited the Fields of the Standing Stones, and there he met Daisybright's sister, whose name was Catkin.

Soon Stumpy and Scab were spending more time in the Field of the Standing Stones with the two young vixens than under the old house with their elders, and in due course they mated.

EIGHTEEN

The Dark before the Dawn

In the world in which they now found themselves, the foxes discovered that early dawn was the best time, especially for those who weren't as nimble as they used to be, or who had other things on their minds . . .

While there were plenty of overgrown gardens in the vicinity of the old house and other areas of dense vegetation close by, Old Sage Brush didn't hunt in them, even at night. Hop-along did, but he didn't go very far. Man's dogs and cats lived all around them, and they knew that a fox that couldn't hop over a high garden wall might find itself in trouble.

Because of this, the two of them would sometimes wait until the darkness was fading and the light was beginning to creep up over the edge beyond the water. Then, accompanied by the vixens, they would go down to the beach. Man, they had discovered, was never around to see the dawn. His dogs, having barked all night, were tired and the cats, having searched the gardens for food and female company, were also curled up, content to leave their hunting ground to others.

As they lay on the rocks, Old Sage Brush would sniff the salty breeze and savour the smell of seaweed. With one ear he would listen to the sound of the sea, and with the other he would listen to Vickey describing the oyster-catchers that frequented the shore.

If the old fox found it difficult to imagine birds the colour of magpies, but with red eyes, orange beaks and pink legs, he was also intrigued by their manner of hunting. He listened with great interest as Vickey told him how they probed the sand for worms, and with great skill extracted small pieces of meat from shells that were also to be found on the shore.

Curiosity, and the pleasure of seeing these birds flying off at his approach, often took Hop-along out to the water's edge. On one occasion he brought back a shell and while he and the old fox examined it, Vickey and She-la talked about other things – things that were the concern of vixens.

'I'm sure you're pleased Scab has found a mate,' said Vickey.

She-la nodded, and confided, 'I've worried a lot about him. The itch and the fire left his fur in such a mess.'

'Catkin seems to see nothing wrong with it.'

She-la smiled. 'That's true, and Daisybright doesn't seem to be worried that her mate has no tail!'

Vickey was silent for a moment, before confessing, 'I'm a bit worried about Sinnéad. She hasn't gone up to see them.'

She-la glanced at Sinnéad who was scratching at seaweed on the rocks, and said, 'I know. I think it's the cat. It seems to remind her of all the things she wants to forget.'

Vickey nodded. 'And what are we going to do about Needle Nine? It's time he found a mate.'

She-la agreed. She knew the mating season was almost past.

Having succeeded in forcing open the shell, Hop-along found the morsel of meat inside a bit salty, even gritty. Old Sage Brush didn't find it much to his liking either, and they decided it was something that was better left to the birds.

When they had returned to their den under the house, Old Sage Brush called Black Tip aside. 'Where's Needle Nine?' he whispered.

'Up on the hill.'

'He seems to be spending a lot of his time up there.'

The old fox paused. 'He wouldn't have found a little vixen by any chance?'

Black Tip shrugged. 'I wouldn't be surprised. Why?'

'Vickey's worried about him. Thinks he should have found a mate by now.'

'Don't worry,' said Black Tip. 'He will.'

Knowing that the old fox was asking him to make sure Needle Nine was all right, Black Tip turned and slipped away. He could understand the old fox's concern. Vickey's too, for Needle Nine had been slower to mature than Stumpy or Scab. Having been reared by man, he had been late in learning the ways of the wild. Then he had almost been choked to death by man. That in itself would have been enough to give any young fox a set-back. Yet he had made an amazing recovery, and somehow Black Tip suspected that food wasn't the only thing that was drawing him up to the hill at dawn.

When Stumpy and Scab had gone to live with their vixens in the Field of the Standing Stones, Needle Nine had experienced a great loneliness, and when the others had gone out to hunt or watch the oystercatchers, he had got into the habit of going up to the hill. There he would lie on the bare rocks at the top, look out over the sea and dream of the young vixen whose scent he had found in the surrounding gorse.

In spite of all the houses that were round about him, Needle Nine could see that where they had settled was still quite a wild place. Up behind him was a hill on the top of which grew evergreens, beyond that a stony hill, the lower slopes of which were covered with leafless trees. Sometimes he would see the great green cater-pillar appearing as if from nowhere, and go creeping around the bottom of the hills. At one stage it went under the ground so that for a time he could only see its head and tail. Somehow it didn't seem so big from where he lay and all the time it carefully avoided the water that rolled gently in to the shore.

When the train had disappeared he would listen to the small birds singing in the gorse and scrub nearby and watch the rays of the sun reaching down through patches of dark rain clouds, to play games with the water. These great fingers of light, he noticed, always turned the water to silver, so that it sparkled until it almost dazzled him

Then other parts of the water began to change colour too, turning from dark green to light green, while the gulls wheeled and turned and screamed as if they knew rain was coming and they didn't like it.

Now and then a ship would make its way slowly across his line of vision and as his eyes followed it out of sight, they would come to rest on a distant mountain. It was the great peak Whiskers had used as a landmark, and he wondered if the mate Whiskers had found at the Edge of the World was now expecting cubs. He also wondered if the little vixen he knew to be close by would be interested in him.

Needle Nine was thus deep in thought when Black Tip saw him lying on top of the small rocky hill. He was about to approach his young friend when he noticed another fox curled up on a grassy bank nearby. He smiled, for he could see it was a little vixen. Quietly he turned and made his way back to the old house.

Because of their preoccupation with Daisybright and Catkin, Stumpy and Scab seldom called to the old house. Perhaps they also knew from the way Sinnéad would get up and go that she got the smell of cat from them, and the last thing they wanted to do was upset her. Vickey, on the other hand, soon overcame her aversion to cats, and in the course of their nightly travels, She-la and herself would call into the Field of Standing Stones. In that way the two young dog foxes learned that their friend, Needle Nine, had found a mate.

'She's lovely,' said Vickey.

'What's she called?' asked Daisybright.

'Ladybird,' She-la told her. 'She's about the same age as yourselves.'

Catkin smiled. 'Yes, we know her. She is lovely.'

While everyone else seemed to be preoccupied with cats and cubs, Old Sage Brush was preoccupied with thoughts of his own. By and large he was happy, for all that Whiskers had promised had come true. Man and his dogs didn't bother them, and as there were no sheep in the area, the grey crows that occasionally landed on the rocks at the water's edge brought no trouble upon them As far as choking hedge-traps were concerned, they were a thing of the past, and the cats that hunted in the gardens were usually easy enough to avoid.

For a blind fox, however, a strange territory presented its problems. Gone were the familiar paths he knew back in the Land of Sinna; gone were the scents and sounds by which he could make his way with the quiet confidence that so often surprised his sighted friends. The visits to the water's edge at dawn with Hop-along and the vixens helped ease the problem, but still he longed to be able to go out on his own, to regain that independence he enjoyed back at Beech Paw.

Had he discussed the matter with any of the others, they would have told him that in time he would get to know the area, find paths that were safe and tread them just as surely as those that allowed him to live in safety in the bog of the birches. All this he knew to be true. Yet he was also conscious of what he had said to the others when they had stopped to rest beneath the great peak.

'For those that are young and fast,' he had told them, 'time moves slowly. But for those that are old and slow, time moves fast.'

Time, he knew, was not on his side, so one night when the others were either asleep or hunting, he slipped out from under the old house and tried to come to grips with this strange new world to which he had brought them.

It was in the old fox's mind that he would start by going down to the beach. This he succeeded in doing, and feeling rather pleased with himself, was making his way back along the bottom of a stone wall when he got the scent of a cat ahead of him. From the strength of the scent he could tell it was a tom-cat, and knowing how vicious tom-cats could be, he considered it prudent to turn with the wall when he felt it branching off. The cat followed, forcing him to make various other turns, and when, eventually, it went its own way, he knew he was lost. He could of course, have followed the scents back to the spot where he had met the cat, but he also knew there was the very real danger that it might by lying in wait for him.

From the Edge of the World a clap of thunder rolled in across the water. Old Sage Brush decided to keep going, and after searching around came upon what he took to be an earth.

There were great heaps of soil around the entrance, and while he could discern no scent of badgers, he decided it must be one of their setts. He could feel spots of rain in the air now, so he made his way down until he was inside.

Shortly after Old Sage Brush had left their den, Sinnéad arrived back at the house. Hop-along was asleep, and she immediately wakened him to ask where her father had gone.

Hop-along shook his head. 'I don't know.'

'What about the others?' she asked. 'Would he have gone with any of them?'

'They had all gone,' said Hop-along. 'There was only the two of us left. I must have dozed off. Sorry.'

'It's not your fault if he's decided to go out on his own,' Sinnéad assured him. 'But he's asking for trouble if he has. He doesn't know his way around here – not the way he does at Beech Paw.'

Hop-along was wide awake now. 'Do you think we should go and look for him?'

Sinnéad shook her head. 'No. You go up as far as the Field of the Standing Stones. Tell Stumpy and Scab. I'll see if I can pick up his scent. He might be all right – but then again, he might not.'

As Hop-along hobbled off, Sinnéad cast around. Beyond the tangle of scents that criss-crossed the garden, she located the one she was looking for and followed it. After a short distance it became obvious that the old fox had taken the path to the shore, so she quickened her pace in the hope of catching up with him. Near the stone wall where he had been forced to turn away from the path by the presence of the tom-cat, she cast around again. Finding that the scents here merged, she realised immediately what had happened, and fearing that the tom-cat might maul him, set off after them as quickly as her nose would allow.

There was thunder in the air now, and a touch of rain in the wind. Afraid that the rain might wipe out the scents, Sinnéad hurried through a maze of lanes and back streets. At every turn she expected to come upon the torn body of the old fox, and thought what a terrible tragedy it would be, what a dreadful irony, if the one who had dreamed of this haven should be the first to die in it.

Emerging from a side street, she found to her relief, that the two scents finally parted. The cat had discontinued the chase, preferring to remain in the shadows, while the old fox, who was always in darkness, had continued across the street to a place where there were heaps of soil and a hole in the ground. There was no scent of man around the hole that she could detect, but there were other things that showed it to be the work of man, things the old fox would not have seen.

Sinnéad looked back. There was no sign of any of the others coming, and hoping that Hop-along had succeeded in alerting them, she moved down into the hole. It was, she found, big inside, bigger even than those dug by badgers. A dribble of water ran along the bottom of it, but apart from that it was dry and the scent of the old fox was strong. Raising her head, she screamed to let him know she was following. Her scream echoed through a maze of tunnels, and when he didn't reply a great sense of foreboding came over her.

Old Sage Brush hadn't gone far when he also came to the conclusion that what he was in was man-made. Apart from the absence of badgers and their scents, the side-chambers showed no traces of habitation. There was, moreover, a distinct smell of man and his waste in some of the tunnels. Turning to retrace his steps, he followed his scent until he realised he must be going around in circles. He stopped, and was wondering what to do when another scent came to his nostrils. It was a scent that was accompanied by shuffling and squeaking – furtive noises that suggested a gathering of creatures who could only find courage in numbers. It was then he knew he was being watched by rats.

When, moments later, Sinnéad's scream echoed through the tunnels, the old fox decided not to answer. He knew well the danger he was in, and the last thing he wanted was to draw her into it.

Edging her way forward, Sinnéad also became aware of the presence of rats. She could detect movements in the shadows and knew they were watching her from numerous cracks and holes. Soon her eyes became accustomed to the darkness, and she could see them. Some of them were sitting at openings, eyes wide, noses twitching, others were scurrying around, disappearing into the shadows at her approach, only to re-emerge farther on – or behind.

Sinnéad was wondering which way to go when an agonising squeal of pain pierced the silence. When it died down, she could hear the chickering of a fox, followed by the squeaks of excited rats and the chopping of teeth, and she knew the old fox was in trouble. The rats that had been watching her could read the sounds just as well as she could. They immediately tumbled into the tunnel ahead of her, and streamed in the direction from which the sounds had come. Racing after them, she turned a corner to find the old fox hissing and chickering as, with teeth bared, he snapped at random in a vain effort to ward off a horde of tormentors he could not see.

Regardless of the danger to herself, Sinnéad charged in and standing back to back, father and daughter snapped and chopped, killing all the rats they could, but taking many a bite themselves.

The rats retreated and regrouped. Sinnéad was panting and she could taste blood on her lips. 'Are you all right?' she asked.

'Well, at least I'm still alive,' the old fox replied. 'But maybe I should have paid more attention to Ratwiddle.'

Sinnéad nodded grimly. The words of Ratwiddle were running through her mind too. 'I have seen the rats hunting the fox,' he had told them back a Beech Paw, and now they were.

The noise of battle and the smell of blood were bringing rats from all sorts of nooks and crannies now. Fortunately, only so many of them could face the foxes at one time. Nevertheless, Sinnéad could feel herself weakening and knew her father must be on the point of collapse. When that happened, he would be dead, and so would she.

As these thoughts went through Sinnéad's mind, she was tempted to turn around and see how the old fox was. At the same time she knew the rats were getting ready to attack again, and that if she did turn, they would be upon her in an instant. She wondered if death would come quickly, or if they would be eaten alive. The thought of such an ignoble and agonising end, not only for herself, but for her father, spurred her on to another frenzy of snapping and biting. For a moment it seemed her determination had paid off, as some of the rats fell back and scurried into their holes.

Surprised at the apparent success of her attack, Sinnéad looked up and to her delight saw two other foxes coming down the tunnel. 'It's Daisybright and Catkin!' she told her father. 'Hop-along must have told them.'

Chopping any rats that dared to stand in their way, the two young vixens tossed them aside without so much as a glance to see if they were alive or dead. Taken off guard, the remainder of the rats scattered, and before they knew what had happened, there were four foxes where only moments before there had been two.

When the young vixens had taken up positions, one on either side of them, Sinnéad sank to the floor of the tunnel. Able to turn around now, she saw that the old fox was bleeding from numerous bites to the lips and face. Tears welled up in her eyes, and she couldn't speak.

'You shouldn't have come down here,' Daisybright told them.

'It was my fault,' whispered Old Sage Brush. 'I thought it was an earth.'

The rats were gathering again, and Sinnéad braced herself for another attack. She could see they were being more cautious this time, probably, she thought, because there were more foxes to contend with. Or was it because they got the smell of cat from the newcomers? She wasn't sure. All she knew was that they were hanging back, watching and waiting . . .

Unknown to the foxes or their attackers, a much greater force was now at work. It, and it alone, would determine what would happen next in the tunnel, for it was about to send a greater enemy rushing down towards them.

Up on the street the storm had broken. Thunder and lightening was tearing the sky apart, and dark clouds were releasing a deluge of rain. The rain hammered on the streets and flowed along the sides of the footpaths. It swirled into gratings and formed a huge torrent that sent the sewer rats scurrying for heights that only they knew existed. The foxes ran, only to find that there was nowhere to run, and before they knew what was happening they were being swept along in a mixture of storm water and human waste. Paddling in a desperate effort to keep their heads above the water, they could feel it pouring in from all directions. Soon the sliver of air above them narrowed to nothing and they were sucked into utter darkness, twisting, turning, unable to breathe. There was taste of salt on their tongues before another darkness enveloped their minds, and they floated off into a state of semi-consciousness where all their troubles were left behind and the chasm that lay beyond the Edge of the World opened up before them.

A short time later, Sinnéad opened her eyes. Gasping for air, she could see she was in the water opposite the shore where she and Old Sage Brush and some of the others had watched the oystercatchers. Some distance away she saw Daisybright and Catkin coming to the surface. Frantically she looked around and waited to see if the old fox would surface.

Bubbles were coming up all around her, but of the old fox there was no sign.

On returning to their den beneath the house, Vickey and the others had found Hop-along in a state of great anxiety, and were alarmed to learn that the old fox had ventured out on his own. Their alarm was heightened by the fact that it was now raining heavily. The rain, they knew, would wash away his scent and he wouldn't be able to follow it back.

Going over to the entrance, Vickey listened to the water as it gushed from the gutters and flowed across the cement path outside. 'Maybe Sinnéad was able to pick it up and find him before it started to rain,' she said.

'She asked me to go up to the Field of the Standing Stones and tell the others,' said Hop-along. 'Stumpy and Scab were out, but Daisybright and Catkin said they would go and have a look for him.'

Black Tip nodded. 'Good. They know the area better than any of us.'

'I wonder what got into him?' said She-la.

Vickey shook her head. 'Who knows? Maybe he just got tired of being cooped up in here all the time.'

'And he didn't say where he was going?' asked Skulking Dog.

Hop-along shook his head. 'He didn't say anything. When I woke up he was gone.' He hobbled over to where Vickey was standing and looked out at the rain-swept night. He knew that without a scent to follow, they were as helpless as he was.

As Sinnéad paddled around in the water, she was vaguely aware that the storm was passing and that the first streaks of dawn were in the sky. Having failed to locate Old Sage Brush, she glanced again at Daisybright and Catkin. They had almost reached the shore, and now for the first time she could see they had something between them. Realising that it must be the old fox, she paddled after them for all she was worth. Several times she was caught in the ebb and flow of the waves before the sea finally decided to release her and cast her up on the shore. By this time, the young vixens had pulled the old fox out, and were standing over him. Staggering across to them, she saw his limp body lying in the sand.

'Is he . . . ' she asked, afraid to complete the question because of what the answer might be.

'No,' replied Daisybright. 'He's still breathing.'

The three of them began to lick the life back into the old fox, and after a while he began to splutter and cough.

Sinnéad heaved a sigh of relief, and lying down beside him put her nose to his, saying, 'You're going to be all right. You're safe now.'

She could see he was covered in cuts and bites and knew from the way her own wounds were smarting, that the salt water must be adding greatly to his pain.

The old fox coughed again, and after a few moments succeeded in pushing himself up on to his belly. 'What happened?' he croaked.

'We were washed into the water,' Catkin told him. 'I think it must have been the rain.'

226

'And what about the rats?'

'They're used to the water,' said Daisybright. 'But they'll know they were in a fight.'

The old fox managed a smile. 'I think these old bones of mine will know it too.'

Behind them the gulls were circling over the spot where they had come to the surface, waiting for anything else that might pop up. The oystercatchers were waiting to see what shells the outgoing tide would leave behind, and none gave more than a passing glance at the four foxes that made their way up the shore. Man, of course, would have been much more interested, but it was still only dawn and he was asleep.

NINETEEN

Dreams of Sinna

In the days that followed, Old Sage Brush and Sinnéad gradually recovered. The salt that had added to their pain, had also cleansed their wounds and allowed them to heal without infection. While the old fox would lie in their den beneath the house, dozing, Sinnéad would curl up in a secluded corner of the garden, and dream. She never told the others what she was dreaming, not even Skulking Dog. All they knew was that after her encounter with the rats, a strange contentment had come over her, and they were happy to see it.

None of them, not even Old Sage Brush, could have guessed that in her day-dreams Sinnéad was casting her mind back to the Land of Sinna . . . She would think of the time the cats had stolen three of her new-born cubs and how they had driven them from the evergreens, and she would dream that perhaps they had missed one, a cat that was deformed in such a way that it couldn't run, a cat that couldn't have kittens.

It had, she dreamed, raised the cubs as its own, and given them beautiful names, Catkin, after herself, Daisybright and Ladybird. It didn't quite fit, of course, for one of hers had been a little dog cub, but by juggling things around in her head, she made them fit.

Later, when she was well enough, she even made her way up to the Field of Standing Stones. By this time Catkin had found a home nearby with Scab, leaving Daisybright to share her den with Stumpy. The cat stayed on, and once as it groomed Daisybright, just as it would groom one of its own, Sinnéad said to the young vixen, 'Your names are beautiful. What do they mean?'

'When I was a cub,' Daisybright replied, 'my mother told me that my eyes were big and bright like the eye of the daisy that grows in the long grass. So she called me Daisybright.'

'And Catkin.'

'It was her tail. Mother said hers was the first to become long and full, like the catkin on the hazel bush. That was why she called her Catkin.'

'And Ladybird?'

Daisybright shook her head. 'I don't know. She's just a friend.'

Sinnéad smiled. 'Your mother had very good taste.'

Daisybright nodded.

Sinnéad looked at the cat which was now grooming one of Daisybright's ears with loving care. She was tempted to ask, 'Who was your mother?' but didn't. Somehow she preferred to dream.

Daisybright was the first to have her cubs; Catkin was next; then Ladybird. And in the way that foxes do, the vixens that didn't have cubs helped those that did. Even the other dog foxes were known to visit them, and when in the middle of the night, Old Sage Brush would slip out of the den beneath the house, no none asked him where he was going. They knew he was well able now to find the Field of Standing Stones on his own.

Gradually the winter at the Edge of the World turned to spring. The birds began to sing. The buds on the willows bulged with gold like the pollen on a bumble bee's legs, and bushes and flowers became a blaze of colour. Hardly had one colour gone when another blossomed to take its place, and sometimes it seemed, at least to the foxes, that the Bow in the Cloud had come to rest on their bright new world.

Soon the days grew warmer and the cubs grew stronger. Swallows swept in over the water and perched on the wires with the housemartins. Later, when summer was at its height, swifts arrived, soaring and swooping as they fed on the wing. The young foxes of course, were too engrossed with their cubs to see such things, but the older foxes saw them. They also noticed that the swifts never came to sit with the swallows or the housemartins. When they asked the old fox why, he suggested that perhaps the swifts had spent so long on the wing they had forgotten how to use their legs. It was then they realised the 'legless' ones he had spoken of had arrived, and it was time to go.

From now on, the Edge of the World would be home to Stumpy, Scab and Needle Nine. With a touch of noses that wished them and their vixens well, Vickey and Black Tip, Sinnéad and Skulking Dog, She-la and Hop-along set their eyes on the great peak and, accompanied by Old Sage Brush, returned to the Land of Sinna.

Author's Note

Towards the end of the 1980s, public opinion turned against the wearing of animal furs, and this brought to an end a decade in which the fox was hunted extensively for its fur in Ireland and Britain. In 1986-87, for example, 63,784 fox pelts were exported under licence from the Republic of Ireland.

Of these, 37,632 were from the wild, the remaining 26,152 were farmed. By 1988–89, exports had fallen to 9,327: 6,902 from the wild, 2,425 farmed.

Thus the pressure on the fox, which at one time had given rise to fears that it might be wiped out in Ireland, eased and they began to become more numerous again. However, this coincided with another development. In the same decade, sheep production had been building up under the EC's Common Agricultural Policy, so that by December 1989 sheep numbers in the Republic had reached a record 5.8 million. With access to other European markets guaranteed, lambs had become a very valuable commodity, and soon there were complaints about the predations of the fox.

Farmers I spoke to had no doubt that they had lost lambs to the fox, and were not inclined to agree with wildlife experts who had concluded that the damage done to healthy lambs by foxes was much less than generally believed.

Be that as it may, some of the foxes in this story realised that it was time they were on their way again. The badgers decided to go with them because many of their species were being killed both officially and unofficially in the Republic in the belief that they were transmitting tuberculosis to cattle.

As for the third animal that features in this story, there was a welcome development in the Republic in 1990 when it was announced that licences to hunt otters would not be issued and none has been issued since. The Wildlife Act was amended in 2000 to give them further protection.

The 'legless ones' referred to by Old Sage Brush, are of course, the swifts. Their scientific name, *apus apus*, meaning 'without a foot', reflects the fact that they lack the full use of their feet and legs. These are small in proportion to the rest of their body, and if they are accidentally grounded, they have little chance of getting airborne again. They can, however, grip vertical surfaces with their four needle-sharp claws which all point forward, and this enables them to nest under the eaves of houses, usually in the older parts of towns and cities.

The animal referred to by Old Sage Brush as a jennet is well known in rural Ireland. It is the offspring of a horse stallion and a female donkey. However, the name given for it in the Oxford dictionary is a hinny. According to Chambers Encyclopaedia, it is sterile because of the differences in the chromosomes of the parents. A cross between a male donkey and a horse mare is a mule.

I would like to thank all those who helped me when I was researching and writing this book, especially my wife, Fran, and my daughters, Michelle, Amanda, Samantha and Simone.

Tom McCaughren, 2007